"You're a single parent, I believe."

She frowned at the sharpness of his question. "Yes, but—" she began.

"Let's get one thing straight then, Mrs. Richards." Jay's voice was taut. "I don't care what Mrs. Roberts may have told you. I'm not in the market for either a mother for Heather or a second wife for myself."

Claire felt her face flame with furious resentment. Surely he didn't think she'd invited Heather to play with Lucy as a step toward getting to know him better? But, yes he had.

Before she could reply he demanded harshly, "Have I made myself clear, Mrs. Richards?"

"Explicitly," she bit out. "I assure you I'm no more in the market for a husband than you are for a wife—a man in my life is the last thing I want!"

PENNY JORDAN was constantly in trouble in school because of her inability to stop daydreaming—especially during French lessons. In her teens she was an avid romance reader, although it didn't occur to her to try writing one herself until she was older. "My first half-dozen attempts ended up ingloriously," she remembers, "but I persevered, and one manuscript was finished." She plucked up the courage to send it to a publisher, convinced her book would be rejected. It wasn't, and the rest is history! Penny is married and lives in Cheshire.

Books by Penny Jordan

HARLEQUIN PRESENTS

HARLEQUIN SIGNATURE EDITION

Don't miss any of our special offers. Write to us at the following address for information on our newest releases.

Harlequin Reader Service
901 Fuhrmann Blvd., P.O. Box 1397, Buffalo, NY 14240
Canadian address: P.O. Box 603,
Fort Erie, Ont. L2A 5X3

PENNY JORDAN

loving

Harlequin Books

TORONTO • NEW YORK • LONDON
AMSTERDAM • PARIS • SYDNEY • HAMBURG
STOCKHOLM • ATHENS • TOKYO • MILAN

Harlequin Presents first edition May 1988
ISBN 0-373-11075-8

Original hardcover edition published in 1986
by Mills & Boon Limited

CHAPTER ONE

'MUMMY, can Heather come home and play with me and then stay for tea?'

Looking down into the pleading blue eyes of her six-year-old daughter, Claire once again blessed the totally unexpected inheritance from her unknown great-aunt that had made possible her move away from the centre of London to the small village of Chadbury St John.

Lucy had blossomed out unbelievably in the short month they had been here. Already she seemed plumper, healthier, and now she had made her first 'best friend'. The huge block of council flats they had lived in before had not led to any friendships for either mother or daughter. They had been living an existence that had virtually been hand to mouth, and with no way out of the dull misery of such poverty.

And then, miraculously, almost overnight everything had changed. How on earth her great-aunt's solicitors had been able to track her down was a miracle in itself, but to learn that she had inherited her cottage, and with it a small but very, very precious private income, had been such a miraculous event that even now Claire sometimes thought she was dreaming.

'Not today, Lucy,' she told her daughter indulgently. 'Heather's mummy won't know where she is if she comes home with us now, will she?' she reminded her crestfallen child gently.

'Heather hasn't got a mummy,' Lucy informed her quickly, speaking for the brown-eyed little girl clinging to her side. 'She only has a daddy, and he goes away a lot.'

Another quick look at the little girl standing close to her own daughter made Claire aware of several things she hadn't noticed before. Unlike Lucy's clothes, although expensive, Heather's were old-fashioned, and too large. Her fine brown hair was scraped back into plaits, and the brown eyes held a defensive, worried look.

Another victim of the growing divorce rate? Claire wondered wryly. Even here in this quiet, almost idyllic village twenty miles from Bath, they were not immune to the pressures of civilisation.

Everyone in the village seemed to accept her own status as that of a young widow. Her great-aunt had apparently not been born locally but had retired to the village after her many years as a schoolteacher, and had, according to what gossip Claire had picked up in the local post office, been the sort of person who believed in keeping herself very much to herself.

Would she have approved of her? Claire's soft mouth twisted in a tight grimace. Probably not. She had learned over the years that people drew their own conclusions about young girls alone with a baby to support, and that they were not always the right ones. It had been hard work bringing Lucy up alone, but once she had been born there was nothing that could have induced her to part with her. The love she felt for her child was the last thing she had expected ... especially ...

'Mummy, please let Heather come back with us.'
Lucy tugged on her jeans, demanding her attention.

'Not today,' she responded firmly, smiling at
Heather to show the little girl that her refusal held
nothing personal. 'I'm sure that there's someone at
home waiting for Heather who would be very
worried if she didn't arrive, isn't there, Heather?'

'Only Mrs Roberts,' the little girl responded
miserably. 'And *she* won't let me have soldiers with
my boiled egg. She says it's babyish.'

Compassion mingled with amusement as Claire
surveyed the childish pout. Boiled eggs and soldiers
were one of Lucy's favourite treats.

'Mrs Roberts is Heather's daddy's housekeeper,'
Lucy told her mother importantly. 'He has to go
away a lot on—on business—and Mrs Roberts
looks after Heather.'

'She doesn't like me.'

The flat statement was somehow more pathetic
than an emotional outburst would have been. And
the little girl did look unloved. Oh, not in any
obvious way—her clothes were expensive and
clean, and she was obviously healthy—but she was
equally obviously unhappy. But surely the blame for
that rested with the child's father, and not with the
housekeeper? Perhaps he was too involved in his
business—whatever it was—to notice that his child
was miserable.

It was the look of stoic acceptance on the child's
face as she took Lucy's hand and started to walk
away that decided her.

'Perhaps, if Heather doesn't live too far away, we
could walk home with her and ask Mrs Roberts if
she could come to tea,' she suggested.

Two small faces turned up towards her, both wearing beaming smiles.

What manner of father was it who would allow his five-year-old daughter to walk home unescorted? Chadbury St John was only a small village, but it was also a remote one. Children disappeared in Britain every day ... were attacked in the most bestial and horrible of ways ... She ... Claire shivered suddenly, things she didn't want to remember obliterating the warm autumn sun. She had been eighteen when Lucy was conceived. An adult legally, but a child still in so many ways, the adored and protected daughter of older parents who had never taught her that the world could be a cruel and hard place.

They had been killed in a road accident shortly after her eighteenth birthday. She had lost everything then—parents, security—everything.

It had been their intention that she would go on to university after school, but her father's pension had died with him, and the small house they lived in had had to be sold to pay off their small debts. There hadn't been much left. Certainly not enough for her to go to university, even if that had still been possible, but an eighteen-year-old girl struggling with the knowledge that she was an orphan and pregnant doesn't have much time or energy to expend on studying.

Of course she could have had an abortion. That was the first thing the doctor had told her after he had got the truth from her. She had wanted to agree—had intended to—but somehow, when it came to it, she couldn't.

And she had never once regretted her decision to

bear and then keep Lucy. Of course, pressure had been put on her to give her up, but she had withstood it. In those early days she had still had some money left from the sale of the house, but that hadn't lasted longer than the first twelve months of Lucy's life.

The council flat they had been given, its walls running with damp, its reputation for violence and vandalism so frightening that some days Claire had barely dared to go out—these were all in the past now. She felt as though she had stepped out from darkness into light, and perhaps it was her own awareness of what suffering could be that made her so sensitive to the misery of the little girl standing at her side.

The three of them walked to the end of the village, Heather hesitating noticeably once they had left the main road behind.

'Heather lives in that big house with the white gates,' Lucy informed her mother importantly.

Claire knew which one Lucy meant. They had walked past it on Sunday afternoons when they explored their new environment. It was a lovely house, Tudor in part with tiny mullioned windows and an air of peace and sanctuary. One glance into Heather's shuttered, tight face told her that the little girl obviously didn't find those qualities there.

They walked up the drive together, but once they were standing outside the rose-gold front of the house, Heather tugged on Claire's sleeve and whispered uncertainly, 'We have to go round the back. Mrs Roberts doesn't let me use the front door.'

There could be any number of reasons for that,

but even so, Claire frowned slightly. It was, after all, the child's home.

They had to skirt well-tended, traditional flower borders and walk along a pretty flagged path to reach the back door.

There was a bell which Claire rang. They waited several minutes before it was answered by a frowning, grey-haired woman, her lips pursed into a grimace of disapproval as she opened the door.

'Mrs Roberts?' Claire began before the other woman could speak. 'I'm Claire Richards. I've come to ask if it would be all right for Heather to come home with us and stay for tea.'

The frown relaxed slightly. 'I suppose it will be all right,' she agreed grudgingly, summing up Claire's appearance. Her faded jeans and well-worn tee-shirt didn't make her look very motherly, Claire thought wryly. She had been working in their small garden this morning, and she suspected that some of the dirt still clung to her jeans. 'Mind you, her father's expected back this evening, so she mustn't be late.'

'Oh no . . . of course not. He'll want her to be here when he gets home.'

'Oh, it isn't that,' the housekeeper contradicted with what Claire thought was an appallingly callous lack of regard for Heather's feelings. 'No, he'll be bound to be busy when he gets back and he won't want to be bothered with *her* . . .' her head jerked in the direction of Heather. 'Course, her mother should have taken her really, but her new husband didn't want her it seems, so Mr Fraser got lumbered with her. I've told him more than once that she's too much for me to cope with, what with the house as well. He should get married again, that's what he should do. He needs a wife, a man like him. All that money . . .' she sniffed and glowered at Heather. 'Still, I suppose it's a case of once bitten, twice shy. Nuts about that wife of his, he was. Neither of them had much time for *her* . . .' Again she jerked her head in Heather's direction, and Claire, who had been too appalled by her revelations to silence her before, placed an arm protectively around each child and stepped back from the door.

'I'll bring her back after tea. If her father returns before then I live at number five, the New Cottages.'

She was shaking slightly as she bustled the girls away. Both of them were subdued. Claire glanced briefly at Heather. The little girl's head was turned away from her, but Claire was sure she could see tears in her eyes.

Of all the thoughtless, cruel women! And by all accounts Heather's father was no better. Oh, she could imagine that it was hard for a man to be left alone to bring up his child, but that did not excuse his apparent lack of love for her. Mrs Roberts had described him as wealthy, and certainly Heather's home had borne out that assertion. If that was the case, why on earth didn't he hire someone who was properly qualified to look after the child?

They were half way back towards the village when Heather said suddenly in a wobbly little voice, 'It isn't true what Mrs Roberts said. My daddy *does* love me. She only says that because she doesn't like me. My mummy didn't love me, though. She left me.'

Claire had absolutely no idea what to say. All she

could do was to squeeze the small hand comfortingly and say bracingly, 'Well, you and Lucy are in the
same boat, aren't you? You don't have a mummy
and she doesn't have a daddy.'

She had little idea, when she made the comforting remark, of the repercussions it was to have, and
if she had she would have recalled it instantly.
Instead, she saw to her relief that Heather seemed
to have taken comfort from her words, and by the
time they had reached the cottage both little girls
were chattering away so enthusiastically that she
couldn't get so much as a single word in.

She let them play in the pretty back garden while
she watched from inside. A bank statement which
had arrived that morning lay opened on the kitchen
table, and she frowned as she glanced at it. Her
inheritance meant that she was no longer eligible
for state benefits, and her small income barely
stretched to cover their day-to-day living require-
ments. Next year she would have rates to pay, and
the old stone cottage needed new window frames;
there was also, according to her next-door neighbour, a problem with the roof. If only she could get a
part-time job? But doing what exactly? She was not
trained for anything, and even if she had been,
there were no jobs locally; she would have to travel
to Bath.

Pushing her worries to one side, she started
preparing the girls' meal. Her small garden boasted
several fruit trees, and she had spent the weekend
preserving as much of it as she could. Now, when
she had least expected it, she was finding a use for
the old-fashioned homely skills her mother had
taught her. Her mother. Claire stilled and stared

unseeingly out of the window. What would she think if she could see her now?

Claire had not arrived until her mother was in her early forties and her father even older. They had surrounded her in their love, and then with one blow fate had robbed her of that love. When the police came to tell her about her parents' accident she had hardly been able to take it in. They had been going out to dinner with some friends and the car which ran into them and caused the accident had been driven by a drunken driver.

She thought that she had endured as much pain as life could sustain, but six months later she had learned better.

'Mum, we're hungry . . .'

Lucy's imperious little voice was a welcome interruption, and although she pretended to frown, Claire soon got both girls seated at the kitchen table and watched in amusement as they demolished the boiled eggs and thin strips of bread and butter.

Real nursery fare. Her mother had made it for her, too. Just as she had made the deliciously light scones and the home-made jam that Claire too had prepared to follow their first course.

'Mrs Roberts never makes any cakes,' Heather complained, happily accepting a second scone. 'She doesn't even buy them. She says sweet things are bad for me.'

Mrs Roberts was quite right, Claire thought wryly, but she prided herself on the methods she used to adapt her mother's recipes to fit in with her own more up-to-date awareness of what was healthy and what wasn't.

She considered that children at six years old still

needed the calcium supplied by unskimmed milk, and she poured them both full glasses, watching the childishly eager way they gulped it down. Heather spilt some and instantly her small body froze, her eyes widening in fright and tension, fixed on Claire's face.

'Don't worry about it, it'll soon wipe up,' she told her cheerfully, trying to hide her shock at the little girl's frightened reaction. Wasn't she ever allowed to spill anything? She was, after all, only a very little girl, but Mrs Roberts hadn't struck her as the type of woman who would make allowances for a six-year-old, and by all accounts Heather's father was too engrossed in his business to notice or care what was happening to his child.

Mentally she contrasted Heather's life with Lucy's. Lucy might lack things in the way of material possessions, but her daughter had never doubted that she was deeply loved. Watching Heather, Claire was fiercely glad that she had never allowed herself to be persuaded to give her child up. Both she and Lucy had lived in poverty, and it had been very hard, but Lucy had never looked at her with such fear and dread in her eyes, and she promised herself that she never would.

Heather was a much less stalwart child—shyer, and more withdrawn; in Lucy's company she seemed to blossom, but whenever Lucy moved out of sight she withdrew into herself again, staring wide-eyed at Claire while she moved about the kitchen.

'Lucy, you've got a spare toothbrush,' she instructed her daughter briskly when they had finished their meal. 'Take Heather upstairs and both of you wash your hands and clean your teeth.'

The cottage was only small, with a sitting-room and a dining-kitchen. Upstairs they had two bedrooms and a tiny bathroom, but after the grimness of the London flat it was sheer bliss to look out of the windows and see the mellow lushness of the Cotswold countryside. They fronted right on to the main road through the village, but even that was a pleasure to look out on to. The cottages lining the village street had been built during the eighteenth century, in mellow cream stone; all of them had small front gardens, filled with cottage garden plants.

As yet the village hadn't been discovered by commuters, but Claire suspected that that state of affairs wouldn't last long. Most of the younger generation had moved away looking for work. All of her neighbours were old—her great-aunt's generation; the village had no industry, other than the land; there was one general store, the post office and a pub. There was talk of the authorities closing the school, but since it took children from two neighbouring villages also, and was well attended, Claire was hoping that this wouldn't happen. If it did, no doubt Heather's father would be able to send her to a private boarding school, but she . . . She was frowning over this when she heard someone knocking on the front door.

She opened it and looked at the man standing on her front doorstep. He was very tall, so tall that she had to tilt her head back to look at him. The immaculate tailoring of his pale grey suit made her lift nervous fingers to her tangled chestnut hair. She hadn't so much as brushed it since coming in with the girls. His own hair was black, and very thick. His eyes were grey and totally expressionless. They were studying her assessingly, and she felt herself blushing hotly as she realised how closely her old tee-shirt and jeans clung to her body.

It had been such a long time since a man looked at her like that she had lost all awareness of her own sexuality. Now, recognising the way his hard glance rested on her breasts, she felt her whole body tense with immediate rejection. He felt her tension too, she could see it in the way his eyes narrowed thoughtfully on hers.

'I believe you have my daughter here.'

His voice was cool, as though warning her off, but warning her off what? For a moment she was so bemused that she couldn't think.

'Your daughter . . .'

'Yes.' He sounded impatient now, his eyes sharp and cold, as though he had judged her and found her guilty of some unknown crime. 'Mrs Roberts, my housekeeper, informed me that you . . .'

'Oh yes, yes . . . of course. You're Heather's father.' Why on earth was he making her feel so flustered?

'Jay Fraser,' he agreed smoothly, watching her. 'And you are . . .'

'Claire Richards.'

'Mummy, we've cleaned our teeth and . . .'

Lucy galloped down the stairs, coming to an abrupt halt at Claire's side, and staring at the man standing in the doorway. Now it was her daughter's turn to be tongue-tied and wide-eyed, Claire saw, while Heather, who had been behind her, raced up to her father, her face alight with pleasure.

'Daddy, this is Lucy, my best friend,' Heather explained to her father importantly, dragging Lucy forwards for his inspection. 'We had boiled eggs for tea and soldiers, and Lucy's mummy made scones . . .' The babble of chatter suddenly dried up and Claire saw Heather's eyes suddenly go wide and tearful as she added huskily, 'Mrs Roberts told Lucy's mummy that you don't love me, but that's not true, is it?'

It most indisputably was not, Claire recognised, watching the mixture of rage and anguish that darkened the grey eyes as Jay Fraser bent down to pick up his daughter.

Over Heather's head, Claire said impulsively, 'I know it's none of my business, but why don't you get someone else to look after her? She needs——' She broke off when she saw the expression on his face.

The grey eyes had frozen. He stepped inside the small hall and put Heather down.

'Why don't you and . . . and Lucy, go outside and play for a little while while I talk to Lucy's mummy.'

Obediently both little girls did as he instructed, leaving Claire with no alternative but to invite him into her small sitting-room.

Once inside the room, he dwarfed it. He must be well over six feet, Claire thought absently, watching as he took the chair she indicated, sinking down into it in a way that suggested an exhaustion his face did not betray. How old was he? Somewhere in his early thirties, probably. What did he do for a living? He certainly wasn't her idea of a businessman. He looked too fit, too physically hard for that . . .

'I'm sorry you've been landed with Heather,' he said distantly at last, reaching inside his jacket and extracting his wallet. 'If you will . . .'

He was intending to give her money? Claire could hardly believe it. Instantly she was furiously outraged. Why, the man was positively feudal!

'It was no trouble,' she told him tightly. 'Lucy wanted to invite Heather back for tea. I thought it best to check with your housekeeper before I agreed.'

He put his wallet away, but his hard expression didn't relax. 'You're a single parent, I believe,' he said tautly, the sharp question making her frown.

'Yes, but . . .'

'Let's get one thing straight then, Mrs Richards. I don't care what Mrs Roberts may have told you; I'm not in the market either for a mother for Heather, or a second wife for myself.'

It took her several shattered seconds to assimilate the meaning of what he was telling her, but once she had, Claire felt her face flame with furious resentment. What on earth was he trying to imply? Surely he didn't think that she had invited Heather to come and have tea with Lucy as a . . . As a what? As a step towards getting to know him better, and through that . . .

But yes, he had. She could see it in the bleak grey eyes watching her with hard determination. He was a wealthy and successful single man with a young daughter to bring up. No doubt he had been the victim of *some* degree of matchmaking, but that was no reason for him to think that she . . .

The red tints in her chestnut hair weren't there for nothing; her temper, normally well controlled and kept in check, refused to be subdued. She opened her mouth to tell him just what she thought of him and his insinuations, but found the hot words stifled in her throat as he suddenly forestalled her and demanded icily,

'Have I made myself clear, Mrs Richards?'

He was standing up now. Business concluded, interview over, Claire thought acidly.

'Explicitly,' she told him in a voice as cold as his own, a spark of rage intensifying the greeny gold of her eyes. Although she didn't know it, her anger had left a soft flush staining her cheekbones, and had brought a slight quiver to her mouth. She looked more vulnerable than fierce, but since she could not see her own expression shs was unaware of the reason for the cynical and faintly brooding expression in those cold grey eyes,

However, even if she didn't know the reason for it, she knew that it existed and that was enough to make her say bitingly, 'I assure you you have nothing to fear from me. I'm no more in the market for a husband than you are for a wife, Mr Fraser. Believe me, a man in my life is the very last thing I want. Lucy and I are perfectly happy as we are.' Her flush deepened betrayingly as she saw the way he looked around her small and rather shabbily furnished sitting-room, and instinctively her fingers curled into her palms. One of the disadvantages of being only five-foot-one was that people sometimes tended to forget that she was a fully grown adult. The look Jay Fraser was turning on her now was one he might have given a slightly dim adolescent. Maybe her home wasn't much by his standards, but she loved it, and whatever he might choose to think there was no way she would ever want to change it for something like Whitegates.

Her resentment against him incited her onwards.

'If you must know, I invited Heather to come back and have tea with us because I felt sorry for her.'

She had got him on the raw there, she saw with a pleasurable stab of satisfaction.

'Oh, I can see you find that hard to believe, Mr Fraser. Heather might have all the comforts a wealthy father can provide, but a busy businessman doesn't always have time for the little cares and worries of a small child. Mrs Roberts didn't strike me as a particularly sympathetic mother-sub-stitute . . .' She took a deep breath and then rushed on, 'In fact it seemed to me that Heather is frightened of her.'

She saw from the white line of rage circling his mouth that he was furious with her.

'Heather doesn't need your pity,' he told her sharply, 'and now, if you wouldn't mind calling her in for me, I think it's time that both I and my daughter left.'

It was perhaps unfortunate that Heather chose to give her a brief and very shy hug before she left, but there was no way she was going to reject the little girl's hesitant affection, Claire told herself as she bent down to hug her back. She didn't like the bitter glance that Jay Fraser gave her as he took Heather's hand and led her away, but if he thought he could simply walk into her house and insult her the way he had . . .

It was perhaps just as well that tomorrow was Saturday, she reflected later, listening to Lucy's chatter as she got her ready for bed. The little girl was full of her new friend and all the things they were going to do together, happily oblivious to the fact that her new friend's father was probably telling his daughter right at this moment that the friendship was over.

In a way his insinuations were almost laughable. Any sort of involvement with any man was so totally opposite to what she wanted . . .

There had only ever been one sexual experience in her life, and that had led to Lucy's conception, and while Claire loved her child with all her heart, the manner of her conception was something that still caused her nightmares. She had no desire for any sort of intimacy with a man; quite the opposite, and so for her, marriage was something that was completely out. Her fear and abhorrence of sex went very deep and was something she normally avoided thinking about. It was less painful that way.

After Lucy's birth her doctor had suggested some sort of counselling, but she had refused. She hadn't been able to bear to discuss her feelings with anyone. She couldn't even examine them in the privacy of her own thoughts.

On Saturday morning Claire had to call at the post office to buy some more eggs. They were delivered fresh each day from one of the local farms, and were a relatively inexpensive and nourishing source of healthy food for both her and Lucy. Fortunately the little girl adored them, and Claire left her examining the treats on the sweet counter while she went to pay for her purchases.

She was just moving away from the counter when she recognised one of her neighbours standing in the queue behind her—nothing moved quickly in the post office; it was the local centre for receiving and sorting gossip.

Her neighbour was an overweight, untidy woman in her late sixties with a faintly overbearing manner. She had come round to introduce herself just after they had moved in, and had almost immediately informed Claire that she was likely to have a problem with her roof. It seemed that most of the cottages had had their roof timbers and slates replaced the previous winter, and that Claire's had been one of the few that had not. She herself had already noticed several loose slates, and she was still worrying about the horrendous expense that would be involved.

Now Mrs Turner smiled eagerly at her and commented in a loud voice, 'Wasn't that the little Fraser girl I saw you with yesterday? Poor little scrap; I feel so sorry for her, poor little mite, rattling around in that great big house, with no one but Amy Roberts for company. And she's never been one for children. Of course, her father really should get married again. She needs a mother, that's as plain as the nose on your face.'

Speculation gleamed in the pale blue eyes, and Claire had to fight down an impulse to be rude to her.

'Heather and Lucy are at school together,' she said instead, forcing what she hoped was a careless smile. 'You know how it is with little girls of that age: a new "best friend" every week.'

She knew quite well that the entire queue was listening, and she only hoped that they picked up the message she was giving out. She could just imagine Jay Fraser's reaction if it got back to him that they were the subject of village gossip.

Luckily Lucy had grown bored with the sweet tray, and so Claire was able to escape from the shop.

It was a pleasantly warm late summer day and she intended to spend it working in the garden. The old lady who lived next door to her had complained during the week that she no longer had the energy to maintain her own garden, and Claire had tentatively offered to take charge of it for her.

In response, Mrs Vickers had thanked her and agreed, but had insisted that Claire had her pick of the raspberries and plums.

For lunch, Claire had made Lucy's favourite ice cream with some of their own strawberries, and on an impulse she took a covered bowl of the sweet round to her older neighbour.

Knowing how proud and independent older people could be she was touched by the enthusiasm with which Mrs Vickers accepted her gift.

'Home-made ice cream—I love it,' the old lady told her with a shy smile. 'My stepmother used to make it for us . . .' She sighed faintly. 'Why is it that the older one gets, the more one returns to the past? There were five of us, you know, three girls and two boys. Our mother died having a sixth. When our father first brought Mary home and told us she was going to be our new mother I hated her. She was less than fifteen years older than I was myself, but she was so patient with us, and so kind. Very modern in her ways too. She insisted that my father let us girls stay on at school, and never made us do more in the house than the boys—and housework was hard in those days. She had three children of her own to look after as well as us five. All that washing . . . and the cooking! My father used to come home for his lunch, and he expected a three-course meal on the table . . . and another at night. But she was always cheerful. I see you had young Heather Fraser round yesterday. Poor little thing. If ever anyone needed mothering it was her.'

Claire, who had been listening to the old lady's reminiscences with interest, tensed slightly.

'Heather has a mother, Mrs Vickers,' she pointed out coolly.

'She has someone who calls herself her mother,' corrected Mrs Vickers stubbornly. 'Never gave a thought to her from the moment she was born, she didn't. Always off out, leaving the baby with anyone she could get to look after her, and once she met that American . . . Many's the time her father's come into the village to buy the poor child something for her tea because her mother'd gone out without feeding her.'

'I really don't think you should be telling me any of this, Mrs Vickers,' protested Claire, softening the words with a smile. 'Mr Fraser didn't strike me as the kind of man who would like the thought of people gossiping about him.'

'Gossip is part and parcel of village life; when you get to my age it's one of the few pleasures left. He did take it very hard when she left, though, and that's a fact. Never seemed to have seen it coming like the rest of us. Of course, with him being away so much . . . He has a manufacturing company in Bath and they do a lot of business abroad. I'm not sure what they make, but she was the sort of woman who needs a man's constant attention, and when he wasn't there to give it to her she looked for it somewhere else. She never struck me as the sort who was suited to village life—or to marriage, come to think of it. Little Heather was only a few months old when they moved in. That father of hers ought to find someone better to take care of her than Amy Roberts, though. Not keen on kiddies, isn't Amy . . .'

That was the second time today that someone had made that observation, reflected Claire a little later as she returned home, and it was one she agreed with. However, the person they should be telling wasn't her but Heather's father. It seemed ridiculous that one brief visit should give the village the idea that in some way she was responsible for Heather's welfare. Nothing like this had ever happened in the block of flats; no one cared or noticed there who went in or out of someone else's front door. But here it was different . . . people did care, and they certainly noticed!

CHAPTER TWO

CLAIRE herself had not expected that Lucy would receive an invitation to have tea with Heather, but it was very difficult to explain to her little girl why she could not bring her new friend home with her every afternoon.

'But Mummy, Heather likes it with us,' Lucy protested one afternoon when Claire had gently but firmly refused once again to allow Heather to come home with them.

'Lucy, Heather has her own home, and her daddy will be waiting for her.'

Privately Claire thought it was appalling that the little girl should be left to walk home from school on her own, and she had got into the habit of walking Heather to her own gates first and then taking Lucy home. From her own point of view she was more than happy to feed Heather *every* tea time; she always had plenty, and the two little girls played happily together. She didn't want Lucy to grow up as a lonely only, and since she herself was never likely to have any more children, friends were something she wanted Lucy to have plenty of.

It tore at her heart to see the woebegone and hurt expression in Heather's eyes, but how could she explain to a six-year-old that she couldn't encourage her visits because her father would put the wrong interpretation on them—not to mention half the village. She did notice, however, that Heather was

26

losing weight and gradually becoming worryingly withdrawn.

Two weeks after her confrontation with Jay Fraser, Claire relented and agreed that Heather could stay to tea the following day, provided that Mrs Roberts agreed.

Everything went very well until it was time to take the little girl home, and then to Claire's dismay Heather burst into tears and clung to her, sobbing pitifully.

'I don't want to go back,' she wept. 'I want to stay here with you and Lucy!'

'But Heather, your daddy . . .'

'He's gone away again. I wish I could come and live with you and Lucy and then you could be my mummy and Daddy could be Lucy's daddy . . .'

'Yes, Mummy, don't you think that would be a good idea?' Lucy piped up. She had gone very quiet when Heather started to cry, but now her brown eyes sparkled excitedly, and the unmistakable contrast between her bright, happy daughter and the little wan face of the child burrowing into her lap caught at Claire's tender heart.

She tried to tell herself that it wasn't all Jay Fraser's fault—a man had to work—but surely he could do better for his daughter than to leave her in the care of someone as plainly unfeeling as Mrs Roberts? Even she herself had quailed a little before the older woman's sternness, and she could well imagine the effect it would have on someone as shy and insecure as Heather. She suspected that Mrs Roberts wasn't above bullying the little girl, and, like all bullies, the more frightened Heather seemed, the more bullying she would become.

'Please, can't I stay here tonight?'

If only she could say yes, but she couldn't, and neither could she explain why not.

'Not tonight, Heather,' she refused gently, softening her refusal by adding, 'perhaps another night, if your daddy will let you. Come on now, let's dry those tears and then we'll take you home.'

She could tell that Heather was reluctant to go, but what could she do? She saw her safely inside the gates, but didn't go up to the house with her, mainly because she didn't want to run the risk of running into Jay Fraser, should he have returned.

Later she was to curse herself for that bit of selfishness, but as she watched Heather's small figure trudging miserably towards the house she had no premonition of what was to happen, only a tender-hearted sadness for the little girl's misery.

The following day, when she went to meet them from school, Claire found that both little girls seemed rather subdued. She left Heather after seeing her safely inside the gates to her home, and although Lucy was quieter than usual, there was nothing in her small daughter's silence to worry her.

They had almost reached their own cottage when Lucy suddenly asked, 'Can Heather come and live with us, Mummy, instead of with Mrs Roberts?'

Sighing faintly, Claire shook her head. 'Heather's daddy would be lonely if she came to live with us,' she said by way of explanation. 'Just as I'd be lonely if you went away from me.'

'But Heather's daddy is always away, and she doesn't like Mrs Roberts. She didn't like her mummy either; she was always cross and smacking her.'

Claire was too aware of how Jay Fraser would react if he ever learned that his daughter had been passing on these confidences to encourage Lucy to say any more. His comments to her on the one occasion on which they had met still stung.

She hated the thought that other people besides himself might consider that she was on the lookout for a husband. A man in her life was the last thing she wanted, especially a man with the legal right to share her bed and her body. She felt herself tense, the familiar sense of nausea sweeping through her.

After she had had her tea, Lucy asked if she could go and play in the garden. Claire agreed readily enough; Lucy knew that she was not allowed to go outside its perimeters.

Mrs Vickers had commented to her earlier in the day that soon it would be autumn. She had remarked on the likelihood of autumn gales and the damage they might do to the cottage roofs. Her cottage, like Claire's, badly needed re-roofing, but unlike Claire it seemed that she had enough money put on one side to cover this expense. She had mentioned a sum that had frankly appalled Claire, who had not realised that the age of the cottages and their country setting meant that they had to be re-roofed in the same traditional hand-made tiles as had been originally used.

She hadn't realised how long she had been sitting worrying about the roof until she heard the church clock chiming seven. She went to the back door and called Lucy, frowning slightly as she scanned the garden and realised there was no sign of her daughter.

She was just wondering if Lucy could possibly

have slipped round to see Mrs Vickers, when she suddenly appeared.

The guilty look on her face was enough to alert Claire's maternal instincts. It was her private and most dreaded fear that the same thing that had happened to her might happen to Lucy, and it was because of this nightmare dread that she was so strict about not permitting her to stray outside the garden. Now, however, the guilt in her daughter's eyes made her hesitate before getting angry with her. Her 'Where have you been?' brought a pink flush to Lucy's face.

'I went for a walk . . .'

'Lucy, you know I've told you never to go out of the garden without me. Come on now, it's bedtime.' How on earth could one describe to a six-year-old the perils that lurked behind the smiling mask of friendly strangers?

'Don't be cross, Mummy.' An engaging smile, and a small hand tucked in hers, made her sigh and decide that her lecture would have to await a more propitious occasion.

It was only when she was making Lucy's supper that she noticed that her cake-tin was almost empty. She frowned slightly. She had never forbidden Lucy to help herself to food if she wanted it, but neither had she encouraged her. Lucy was not a greedy child, and rarely asked for food between meals, but she could have sworn that that cake-tin had held far more home-made buns last night than it did now.

Normally Heather was waiting for them outside the school gates, but this morning there was no sign of her, and Claire couldn't help feeling concerned.

Was the little girl ill? Heather wasn't her responsibility, she reminded herself, and neither her father nor Mrs Roberts would thank her for interfering, and yet she knew that if Jay Fraser's reaction to her had been different she would have called at the house on her way home and checked to see if Heather was all right.

She knew that Heather was perhaps becoming too attached to her, needing a mother substitute, and while she had scrupulously tried to avoid encouraging the little girl to depend on her in any way at all, she knew that she herself was growing very attached to her. Heather wasn't her child in the way that Lucy was, but there was something vulnerable in Heather that cried out for love and attention.

Several times during the morning she found herself worrying about her, remembering her wan little face. Heather was frightened of Mrs Roberts, and while she didn't think the housekeeper would go as far as to physically maltreat the child, there were other ways of inflicting pain and fear on children.

She had almost decided that after lunch she would call round at Whitegates and brave Jay Fraser's wrath if he found out, when she heard her doorbell ring.

The sight of Jay Fraser standing on her doorstep, flanked by the village constable and a young women in police uniform, was so shockingly unexpected that she was robbed of breath.

It was the policewoman who spoke first.

'Mrs Richards. I wonder if we could come in for a moment.'

Conscious of the curiosity of her neighbours, Claire hurriedly agreed. Her small sitting-room had never seemed more cramped. The local policeman, although not as tall as Jay Fraser, was still quite large. He was an older man, married with two grown-up sons, and he seemed pleasant. Now however, he looked worryingly grave, and Jay Fraser, who had refused her offer of a seat, looked almost ill. The tan she had noticed on his first visit now seemed a dirty yellow colour. His immaculate white shirt was unbuttoned at the throat, his tie askew, and his hair ruffled.

'Mrs Richards, I believe your little girl is very friendly with Mr Fraser's daughter.'

A terrible sense of foreboding overcame her.

'Yes, yes, she is,' she agreed in a husky voice. 'They're . . . they're best friends.'

All that she constantly dreaded for her own daughter suddenly filled her mind, and it was as though Heather was actually her own child. She sank down into a chair, her body trembling.

'Something's happened to her, hasn't it?'

Sergeant Holmes grimaced slightly. 'We're hoping not, Mrs Richards. We do know, however, that she's disappeared. Mr Fraser's housekeeper reported it to us late last evening.'

'Late last evening?'

'Yes, after the little girl didn't come home from school.' The sergeant frowned, and looked across at Jay Fraser. 'It's probably none of my business, sir, but that's quite a lonely walk home for a six-year-old . . .'

'Mrs Roberts had strict instructions to take Heather to and from school,' Jay said tightly.

In that instant Claire felt for him, truly under-standing how he must be feeling. No doubt he had given the housekeeper her instructions, never imagining that they would be disobeyed. More out of compassion for him than anything else Claire said huskily,

'I . . . I . . . used to walk home with her. I didn't like the thought of her walking alone. It wasn't far out of our way . . .'

Instantly the sergeant's frown disappeared, and he said eagerly, 'And did you walk back with her yesterday, Mrs Richards?'

'Why, yes. I always walked her to the gate and saw her safely inside. I . . .'

She heard the sound that Jay Fraser made and felt her own throat muscles lock in a mingling of pity and fear.

'Then you must have been the last person to see her.' The sergeant frowned. 'Mrs Roberts says that she didn't come home from school last night.'

And the woman had waited how long to report that she was missing? Inadvertently Claire looked across at Jay and saw the same emotions she was feeling reflected in his eyes.

'Mmm. I was wondering if we could talk to your little girl, Mrs Richards. Children sometimes confide things to their friends that they don't tell adults. We won't say anything to frighten her,' he added, correctly interpreting her expression.

'She and Heather were very close,' Clair ad-mitted. She bit her lip and glanced apologetically at Jay. He wasn't looking at her. He was staring down at the carpet, his face set and hard.

'I don't know if it's important, but I know that

Heather was . . . well, she didn't get on very well with Mrs Roberts.'

She caught Jay's roughly expelled breath, and hurried on. 'Of course it might not mean anything . . . and I'm not suggesting that Mrs Roberts was in any way unkind to her . . . but Heather is a very sensitive child.'

'And you think that perhaps she might have said something to upset the little girl? Children of that age get odd notions into their heads,' the sergeant agreed. 'I'll never forget when our boy decided to leave home. All of five he was, and luckily a neighbour found him pedalling down the road on his trike.'

'If Heather had walked off like that someone would have seen her,' interrupted Jay roughly. 'God—she's only a baby . . .' His voice was full of anguish. 'She's been gone all night . . . nearly twenty-four hours!'

Claire felt for him, but she suspected that the last thing he would want would be her sympathy. He must be in hell right now, she thought compassionately. What parent wouldn't be?

'Have you informed her . . . her mother, sir?' Sergeant Holmes asked.

Jay shook his head. 'She wouldn't want to know. I would have given her custody of Heather, but she didn't want her.' His back straightened, his face suddenly bitterly angry, as he read the expression in the policeman's eyes. 'I love my daughter very much, Sergeant,' he told him curtly, 'but that doesn't stop me thinking that a little girl of Heather's age needs her mother. I can't be there all the time for her. God, when I think I deliberately looked for an older woman to look after her, thinking that she would be likely to be more responsible! I have to be away a great deal—there's nothing I can do about it, at least not at the moment . . .'

'No one's blaming you, sir,' Sergeant Holmes said quietly. 'All of us here are parents, and we all know what kids are like. Half the time you just don't know what's going through their heads.'

'If she was so frightened of Mrs Roberts, why didn't she tell me? If anyone's touched her . . . hurt her . . .'

He couldn't put his fears into words, and Claire felt her body clench on a wave of nausea and pain. That was the way *her* father would have looked if he'd known . . . but he'd been dead then and she'd been alone . . . She sent up a mental prayer that somehow Heather would be safe. If she was, no matter what her father had to say about it Claire intended to give her as much love and attention as she wanted. She felt almost as much to blame as Jay. She had known that Heather was unhappy, but because of her pride and her determination not to give Jay the slightest cause to think she was trying to attract him, she had deliberately backed off.

'I normally go and collect Lucy from school about now,' she told the sergeant. 'Do you want to come with me, or shall I . . .?'

'It's best if you go alone; we don't want to frighten her. Try and act as naturally as possible with her, Mrs Richards. Children get some weird ideas in their heads. If she does know anything we don't want to frighten her into keeping it to herself.'

The sergeant's words made sense, but they were

hard to put into practice. Claire could feel her voice turning croaky with anxiety as she casually asked if Heather was at school, already knowing what the answer would be.

Lucy shook her head. As Claire looked down at her, she saw that her daughter was avoiding her eyes.

Did Lucy know something about Heather's disappearance? Striving to seem calm, she said, 'Oh dear, Heather's daddy's waiting for us at home. He thought Heather might be coming home with you.'

No reaction, but Claire felt the small hand tucked into hers clenching betrayingly.

She took Lucy into the kitchen and settled her with a glass of milk and a biscuit before going into her sitting-room.

'I think she knows something,' she told Sergeant Holmes worriedly.

'Will you let me talk to her?' he asked. 'I promise I won't frighten her.'

Knowing what was at stake Claire could hardly refuse. She took the two police officers into the kitchen and made sure that Lucy knew who they were before leaving her with them. She sensed that the sergeant was more likely to learn something if she was not hovering anxiously at his side.

As she opened the sitting-room door she saw that Jay Fraser had slumped down into one of her chairs, his head in his hands. He looked up as she walked in, and she saw the dread and the pain in his eyes.

'I pray to God that we can find her.'

Instinctively she placed her hand over his, shocked to feel its fierce tremble. 'I'm sure Lucy knows something . . . she looked so guilty. Perhaps

Heather's . . .' she broke off, her eyes widening as she suddenly remembered Lucy's disappearance and the missing cakes.

'What is it?'

'I think Heather might have run away,' she said unsteadily. 'Last night Lucy disobeyed me and left the garden . . . I found some cakes missing, I . . .'

Before she could say any more the sitting-room door opened and Sergeant Holmes appeared, holding a tearful Lucy in his arms.

'I promised Heather I wouldn't tell Mummy . . .' her bottom lip wobbled. 'She wanted to come and live with us, but you said she couldn't, and Mrs Roberts was very cross because she'd come here for her tea. Heather wanted her daddy, but he wasn't there . . .'

Oh, the anguish of that innocent double indictment! Over the tousled brown curls, grey eyes met green, both of them mirroring their guilt and anguish.

'It seems that Heather spent the night in one of the huts on the old allotments down by the railway,' Sergeant Holmes informed them. 'She made Lucy promise not to tell.'

'Mrs Roberts smacked her,' Lucy whimpered, 'she made her cry . . .'

'I was wondering, Mrs Richards—if WPC Ames here stays with Lucy, would you . . .'

Claire didn't even think of refusing. After hugging and kissing her daughter and reassuring her that no one was cross with her, she was half way out of the door as Jay opened it.

It was less than half a mile to the allotments, but none of them spoke. All of them must surely be

thinking of the terrors that could be inflicted on a
small girl of six on her own.

As they reached the allotments, the Sergeant
suggested softly, 'I think you'd better be the one to
go first, Mr Fraser. If she's still there, we don't want
to frighten her.'

From the white look on Jay's face, Claire knew
that nothing on earth would have prevented him
from going first. Hands clenched, her body tense
with dread, she waited as he walked towards the
tumbledown hut.

He opened the door and went inside. Claire held
her breath, all sensation suspended as she prayed
harder than she had ever done in her life before. It
was illogical to feel this depth of emotion for
someone else's child, but she knew the horrors that
could be inflicted on the innocent—oh, how she
knew—and in that aeon of waiting there was an
emotional bonding between her personal anguish
and the fear she felt for Heather that coalesced in a
wave of love so strong and intense that when Jay
walked out of the hut, carrying his daughter in his
arms, nothing on earth could have stopped her from
stumbling across the distance that separated them
to take the sobbing child in her arms.

Small arms clung to her, heaving sobs swelling
the childish chest. Jay looked white and stunned—
lost, almost.

'She was frightened of me!' Claire heard him say
disbelievingly. 'She was frightened . . .'

'Let's get her home now,' Sergeant Holmes
suggested, 'time for questions later.'

As Jay leaned forward to take her from Claire,
Heather clung to her, and wept piteously. 'I want to

go to Lucy's house, Daddy. I don't want to go home!'

Claire avoided looking at him. She could sense everything that he was feeling. If he had resented and disliked her before it must be nothing to what he was feeling now.

They took Heather back to the small cottage, a look of relief and guilt mingling on Lucy's face as they walked in.

'I think we should leave her with Mrs Richards for a few minutes, sir,' Sergeant Holmes suggested to Jay.

Busy trying to soothe Heather's tears, Claire was absently aware of Jay stepping back from them and allowing the sergeant to take him into the kitchen.

It was a long time before Heather calmed down enough to be coherent, and the story she told left Claire shaking with rage and appalled by the enormity of what could have happened.

She took her upstairs and put her in the spare bed in Lucy's room, knowing from experience that such an outburst would soon result in sleep. She was emotionally and physically drained, poor little mite, and even in sleep she clung to Claire's hand, not wanting her to leave her.

She went down to the kitchen, where the sergeant was entertaining Lucy by reading her a story.

'She ran away because she was frightened of Mrs Roberts,' Claire told them tiredly. 'It's partly my fault.' She looked at Jay Fraser and saw that his face was shuttered and remote. Who knew what he was thinking behind that iron mask? 'She wanted to have tea with us the other day and I . . . I refused. I said she must ask Mrs Roberts' permission. The next day she said she had; I didn't check—I . . .' She couldn't look at Jay Fraser; surely he must know why she hadn't felt able to speak to his housekeeper. 'Apparently she hadn't asked at all, and after I took her home that evening Mrs Roberts was very angry with her—the poor woman must have been out of her mind with fear when she didn't turn up from school. Apparently she shut Heather up in her bedroom and told her she was going to tell her daddy what she had done. Mrs Roberts told Heather that her father would be very cross.' Claire bit her lip, wondering if she ought to suppress the next bit, and then, deciding that she could not, 'Apparently Mrs Roberts threatened to leave and told Heather that if she did, Heather would have to go into a home because neither her mummy nor her daddy wanted her.' She heard the sound Jay made and steeled herself against it. 'That's why she ran away. She was frightened.'

'I never knew!' It was agony listening to the torment in his driven voice. 'I trusted the woman. I thought she was reliable! I had no idea.'

'It happens to the best of us, sir,' said Sergeant Holmes gruffly. 'Try not to blame yourself. I've known Amy Roberts for years. I knew she did't like kids, but I'd never have suspected . . .'

'I'll have to dismiss her, of course.' Claire felt that he was talking more to himself than to them. He looked directly at her for the first time and she was shocked by his haggard expression.

'Could you . . . would you let her stay here tonight? I'll . . .'

'I'll leave the two of you now, sir. No need for us to stay any longer . . .'

Tactfully the sergeant and his colleague left. Lucy was sitting down in front of the television in the sitting-room when Claire peeped in to check that she was all right.

She went into the kitchen. Jay Fraser was standing by the window, his arms rigid against the rim of the sink. He looked up at her entrance and stepped back from the unit, his movements jerky and unco-ordinated. He walked like a man who had had too much to drink, and suddenly he swayed, his face tinged with a frightening pallor.

'The bathroom,' he muttered thickly.

Numbly Claire told him, trying to blot out of her mind the sound of him being violently sick. Shock affected people in many different ways, and she could almost feel the bitter combination of pain and anguish that made up his.

When he came back down he moved like an old, old man. Leaning against the kitchen door, he said slowly, 'I owe you an apology.' He shuddered suddenly. 'God, when I think of what could have happened to her . . . I had no idea how she felt, no idea at all.'

She could hear and see the anguish of a parent suddenly realising how it had failed its child. Ridiculously, she wanted to comfort him, but what could she say?

'You did your best. It can't be easy . . .'

'No, I didn't do my best,' he said savagely. 'If I'd done my best she'd have a proper mother.' His eyes suddenly focused on her and darkened. 'Someone like you. Have you any idea what it does to me to know that you know more about her feelings and her fears than I do . . .? That you cared enough to

make sure she got home from school safely, while
I . . .'

'You didn't know. You couldn't know. In your
shoes I'd have opted for an older woman.'

'I should have known there was something
wrong. Hell, I *did* know,' he said savagely. 'She
never stopped talking about you, but I wouldn't
listen. It's been one hell of a bad year for me,' he
added slowly. 'The divorce became final eighteen
months ago. I suppose you've heard the story: the
neglected wife leaving; having an affair with her
husband's business partner right under his nose.
Susie never wanted children. She wanted to abort
when she discovered she was pregnant . . .'

He was telling her things he'd normally never
dream of telling anyone, Claire sensed; his defences
were relaxed by shock and fear. He needed the
release of talking, even if he barely realised who he
was talking to. She wasn't a person to him right
now, she was just a presence . . . someone to listen.

'She never cared for Heather, and Heather
seemed to sense it. I was glad when she said she
didn't want her. She's my child and I love her,' he
said fiercely as though she had voiced a doubt. 'But
after my experience with Susie I swore I'd never
marry again; never allow another woman to
entangle me in that sort of emotional mess. It isn't
that easy, though. Human beings have certain
needs.' He wasn't aware of how Claire froze. 'And I
soon discovered there are plenty of women willing
to share a man's bed, especially when they think
he's vulnerable. I've lost count of the number of
women who've told me that Heather needs a
mother.'

He knew who she was now, Claire recognised, catching his oblique glance.

'I misjudged you and I'm sorry for it, but I'd just spent a fortnight in the States, trying to fend off half a dozen or so attempts at matchmaking from the wives of my business colleagues. Heather might need a mother, but I don't want a second wife.' He pushed one hand through his hair. 'What the hell am I going to do?'

What could she say? 'I don't know.'

'Neither do I,' he said grimly.

She heard him sigh as he levered his shoulders off the door. Even now, exhausted with anxiety and tension, there was a magnetic attraction about him that she recognised and recoiled from. She saw him frown as she stepped back.

'Look, I really am sorry about what I said to you. There was no call for it. Put it down to tiredness and the frustration of having to fend off my friends' matchmaking efforts. To have you repeat what they had been saying to me—that Heather needed a mother——'

'Made you leap to the instant conclusion that I had myself in mind,' said Claire wryly. 'Yes, I can understand that, but you were quite wrong. A husband is the last thing I'd want.'

She saw him frown. 'My remark was crass and uncalled for.'

A silence stretched between them, but it wasn't an uncomfortable silence. In fact, it was oddly companionable.

'I'll come and see Heather later, if I may. Will it be all right if she stays here with you?'

She could see how much he hated having to ask,

and that was something else she could understand
from her own experience of single parenthood. It
bred in one a fierce pride, a determination to
manage alone without having to ask for help—but
help was sometimes needed, and it wasn't in her
nature to be anything less than generous. Pushing
the heavy weight of her hair off her face, she said
firmly, 'Heather can stay here as long as she wants
to. I'm genuinely very fond of her, you know,' she
paused, searching for the right words, 'she's so
vulnerable . . . and . . . and wanting. Nothing like
my independent little Lucy.'

'Perhaps because she hasn't experienced the
same security and love.' Jay's voice was clipped, his
eyes edged with bitterness. 'I've got to go back now.
I want to have a few words with Mrs Roberts. I
can't blame it all on her, though; *I* should have
known. But she seemed so responsible. She had
such good references!'

'As a housekeeper, perhaps,' said Claire gently,
sensing his frustration and guilt. 'But a woman
who's a good housekeeper isn't always a good . . .'

'Mother? No,' he said bitterly. 'I can see that—
now. I'll just go up and see Heather before I leave.'

He sounded uncertain and awkward, and Claire
didn't go with him. Some things were too private to
be witnessed by anyone else.

'She's still asleep,' he told her when he came
down. 'I'll come back later.' Claire walked with him
to the front door. As she opened it he turned to face
her.

'I haven't thanked you,' he said huskily.

'There's nothing to thank me for.'

And she didn't feel there was. If she hadn't been

there perhaps Heather might never have thought of running away. She hadn't meant to encourage the little girl to love her, but how much damage had she inadvertently done?

CHAPTER THREE

BOTH girls had had their supper and were bathed and pyjamaed when Jay Fraser came back. They were sharing Lucy's room, but Claire took her own daughter downstairs so that Jay and Heather could be alone.

She had barely been downstairs with Lucy for more than ten minutes when Jay Fraser's dark head suddenly appeared round her sitting-room door. He looked unexpectedly vulnerable for such a very hard-edged men, his mouth set in a grimly despondent line.

'Can you come?' he asked quietly. 'Heather seems to have cast me in the role of angry parent; I can't get it through to her that she isn't going to be punished.'

Claire had always been acutely sensitive to the feelings of others and it was for that reason that she kept her attention fixed on a point to the left of his shoulder rather than on his face. She didn't need a crystal ball to know that he was finding it very hard to ask for her help.

When she got upstairs Heather was curled up in a small ball, crying. The moment she saw Claire she flung herself into her arms, cuddling up against her. Over her dark head Claire looked at the grimly set face of her father. Strange to think that less than a month ago she had viewed a second meeting with this man with both apprehension and dread. Now she was seeing him stripped of his masculine arrogance, a human being with fears and doubts, and ridiculously she wanted to reassure him that everything would be all right, and that Heather would eventually come round.

Instead, she stroked her soft dark hair, and said quietly, 'It's all right, Heather, your daddy isn't cross with you. He was very worried about you, we all were.'

'Mrs Roberts said he would lock me in my bedroom without anything to eat.'

The harsh exclamation smothered in his throat drew Claire's eyes back to Jay's face. She wasn't enjoying witnessing his suffering.

'Mrs Roberts is gone now. Your daddy is going to find someone else to look after you . . . when you go home.'

'I don't want to go home!' Although they were muffled against her breast Heather's words were quite clear, her voice shrill with a mixture of fear and stubbornness. 'I want to stay here with you. I want you to be my mummy.'

Claire didn't dare look at the tense figure standing by the door. What on earth was he thinking?

Swallowing the lump in her throat she said huskily, 'Heather, you know that I love you very much, but I'm not your mummy . . .'

'But I want you to be.' Tears weren't very far away, and Claire gnawed tensely at her bottom lip. What on earth could she say?

The bedroom door opened and Lucy came in, frowning. 'What are you doing up here?' she demanded. Her question was directed at Claire, but she was looking at Jay with a mixture of assessment and fascination in her eyes. To Claire's amazement she went up to him, tilting her head back so that she could look at him. For a little girl who had had virtually nothing to do with the male sex, she was amazingly at ease with him.

'Can Heather stay here with me?' she asked him. 'My mummy could look after her, and we could play together . . .'

Across the room green eyes met grey. 'Lucy, I think it's time that you and Heather were both in bed.'

Claire had a suggestion to make, but she wasn't going to say anything in front of the girls, just in case Jay Fraser rejected it. She wasn't going to be accused of putting him in a position where he couldn't do so.

She tucked Heather up in bed, and bent down to kiss her. Lucy climbed into the other single bed, and after she too had received her goodnight kiss she looked across at Jay and demanded, 'Aren't you going to kiss us too?'

Claire hid a small smile at the expression in his eyes, but he acceded to Lucy's request easily enough, kissing her first and then Heather, who shrank away from him slightly.

Downstairs in the sitting-room she offered him coffee, but he shook his head.

'More stimulation is the last thing I need right now. I've got a feeling it's going to be hard enough to get to sleep as it is, and in less than forty-eight hours I've got to fly back to the States. I'm more in need of a stiff whisky than caffeine.'

'I'm sorry, I don't have any,' Claire apologised,

but he shook his head again.

'I couldn't drink it anyway, I'm driving.'

She wished that he would sit down; he made her feel nervous standing over her like that. It gave her an unpleasant sensation in the pit of her stomach to be alone with him. She always felt like that with men, no matter how harmless they might be. As he moved restlessly she stepped back from him, biting her lip as she saw his frown.

'I didn't want to say anything when the girls could overhear us, but . . . if it would help I could have Heather until you find someone to take charge of her.'

Complete silence followed her offer, and Claire felt the colour crawling over her skin. Surely he didn't still think she had an ulterior motive for making the offer? She risked a look at him, but could read nothing in the slate-grey eyes and hard mouth.

'Look, I assure you that I don't want . . . a husband . . . if that's what you're thinking . . .' She could have cried at her own gaucheness. What on earth must he be thinking? She told herself it didn't matter and that Heather was the prime concern here.

If Jay Fraser had been a woman there wouldn't have been the slightest degree of awkwardness in her making the suggestion, but with his remarks about a second marriage and involvement very much to the forefront of her mind, Lucy hoped that he wouldn't misconstrue her offer.

The silence stretched from seconds into minutes, while her heartbeat picked up to an almost unbearable speed. What on earth was he thinking?

Why didn't he say something, even if it was only a refusal?

When he did speak he sounded very abrupt. 'You make me feel very ashamed of myself,' he told her. 'You're being far more generous than I deserve. Almost every other woman I know would have enjoyed making me eat humble pie and beg for the help you've just offered. It's an art at which my ex-wife was an expert.'

'Do you . . . do you still love her?'

Claire felt her face flame with embarrassment. What on earth had got into her? She looked away from him, and said indistinctly, 'I'm sorry, that was unforgivable.'

'It's all right. You aren't the first to ask. No, I don't still love her. I don't think any man can love a woman who rejects his child. To be honest with you, I no longer believe that passionate love exists. Sexual desire, yes, and non-sexual love of the kind I feel for Heather. And you . . . do you still love Lucy's father . . .?'

She went white and stepped back from him, her eyes huge with pain. It was a natural enough question and he couldn't know how she felt about the man who had fathered Lucy, nor could she tell him. She couldn't tell anyone.

'I . . .'

'Forget it, I shouldn't have asked. I take it there's no chance of the two of you getting back together.'

He had obviously completely misread her reaction, and like someone in a dream Claire said thickly, 'I . . . he's dead . . .'

'Oh, I see. I'm sorry.'

'It . . . it was a long time ago. Before . . . before

Lucy was born.' She was lying. She had no idea whether Lucy's father was alive or dead, or where he was. Or even who he was, a small voice reminded her, but she shuddered with the onset of familiar pain and loathing, forcing her mind to shift from the past to the present, before her memories could overwhelm her. 'About Heather?' she added.

'If she can stay with you for the time being I'd be more than grateful. I'm going to have to get someone to replace Mrs Roberts, of course.'

'There's no need to rush. I'm very fond of Heather.'

'Yes, I can see that.'

'There's something about her that reaches out to me. A need that Lucy doesn't have, a loneliness.' Claire broke off, suddenly conscious of what she was saying.

'Yes, she is lonely,' he agreed bitterly. 'Susie was never much of a mother to her. She never wanted her at all . . .' He too broke off, and Claire sensed that his marriage and his daughter were normally two subjects that he did not discuss with anyone.

It seemed that a strange bond had been formed between them, a bond that at the moment was very tenuous and fragile, and which instinctively Claire feared. She knew that sexually she had nothing to fear from him. A man like Jay Fraser did not need to force himself on a woman.

She watched him as he got up, aware of the way his shirt clung to his shoulders and tapered down to his waist. He was a very masculine man, and the knowledge made her shiver with distaste as she instinctively averted her eyes from his equally masculine stance.

'While Heather is living with you, you must let me make some contribution to your household budget,' he said.

'No.' Her refusal was immediate and firm. 'No, I can't let you do that.'

He frowned and Claire knew that he was a man who did not like to be beholden to others in any way at all.

'If you won't accept money from me, I'll have to find a way of repaying you in kind,' he said at last. He glanced at his watch. 'I'd better go; I'm expecting a call from the States. I'll come round and see Heather tomorrow, if I may?'

Claire saw him to the door, watching as he slid his lean length behind the wheel of his car—a long, low-slung Jaguar sports car. He gave her a brief nod as he fastened his seat belt, and she went inside and closed the door. She was tired now and very drained, but too on edge to sleep. If anything had happened to Heather ... It was almost as though the little girl was her own child. She mustn't get too attached to her or, more importantly, allow Heather to get too attached to her. No, she must gradually reassure her that her father both loved and wanted her; she must instil in her enough self-confidence for her to go back to her father happily and gladly.

When Jay called the following day, she deliberately left father and daughter alone together, but it was Lucy who chatted away to him, demanding that he play, while Heather clung anxiously to her side.

'I was going to suggest that if you could let me know when you're likely to be home I could arrange to bring Heather back to you for those weekends?'

'You think you can manage that, do you?' he

asked sardonically. 'It seems to me that I'm featuring very much as the cruel father at the moment.'

'Only because of what Mrs Roberts has been feeding her. She's been using you as a threat to frighten her. She'll get over it. She does love you, Jay.'

It was the first time she had used his name directly, and she wondered what had caused his eyes to change from light to dark grey like that.

'I'll ring you from the States before I come back.'

It was Lucy who ran up to him for a goodbye kiss, and Heather who had to be gently pushed. Claire's tender heart ached for him, for, despite his controlled smile, she knew that inside he was hurt.

Two months slipped by without Jay being able to find a suitable replacement for Mrs Roberts, and during that time Heather blossomed. She was always going to be a more vulnerable child than her own daughter, Claire thought, but now she looked forward to her father's return, running to him eagerly, and Claire hoped that she had banished the spectre of Mrs Roberts' threats.

October was a cold, wet month with high winds that disturbed the shaky tiles on her roof. Several came crashing down one night as she lay in bed, and she wondered how on earth she was going to pay for them to be replaced.

Jay was due home on Friday. She must remember to go up to Whitegates and turn on the central heating; he had given her a key to the house several weeks ago, but she was scrupulous about using it only when she had to. She had fallen into the habit

of checking on the contents of his fridge when she
knew he was due back, but she had never ventured
further than the kitchen when he was not there, nor
did she linger when she delivered Heather to him,
despite his suggestions that she and Lucy stay and
have a meal.

He didn't make her feel nervous as other men
did; she wasn't frightened of him, and she didn't
know really why she was so anxious to remove
herself from his vicinity. Perhaps it had something
to do with their very first meeting and her
determination that he would never be able to accuse
her of running after him. It was, after all, the last
thing she was likely to do! Her mind might be able
to accept that he was a very attractive and
masculine man, a man with an uncommon degree of
sex appeal combined with that aura of power that
women find so sexually stimulating, but she wasn't
like other women; his sexuality made her cringe.
She found conversation with him stimulating and
interesting, but only if she could manage to blot out
his masculinity. She was glad that he wasn't the sort
of man who liked to touch. She didn't think she
could have endured that.

Mrs Vickers was opening her gate just as Claire
went past with the girls on the way to school.

'Gales forecast for tonight' she warned Claire.
'Hope our roofs will stand up to it.'

Claire did too. When she got back from school
she saw that the row of elms on the opposite side of
the road were swaying fiercely in the strong wind.
All the leaves were gone now, and the branches
looked starkly bleak. Winter would be early this
year.

She spent the morning baking, more for the therapeutic properties of the task than for any real need to provide the girls and herself with sustenance. When she collected them from school, they went first back to the cottage, where Heather sniffed the warm scented kitchen aroma eagerly.

'Have you made an apple pie?' she asked Claire, surveying the fruits of the afternoon's labours enthusiastically.

She had, using the apples from their own tree.

'It's Daddy's favourite. Perhaps we could take him some.?'

On the face of it there was no real reason why they should not; Claire always made something extra when she baked which she normally took round to Mrs Vickers; the three of them on their own would certainly not get through everything she had made—but even so, she hesitated, knowing all too well the construction that Jay could place on her gift of food. However, she knew equally that it was not something she could explain to his six-year-old daughter.

Hating to wipe the happy look of pleasure from Heather's face, she suggested instead,

'Perhaps next time. I made this one for Mrs Vickers. It's *her* favourite too,' childishly she crossed her fingers behind her back as she mouthed the small fib, 'and you can help me make it,' she told Heather. 'I'm sure your daddy would like that.'

'I'll help too,' Lucy chimed in. 'I could make him some of my gingerbread men.'

Claire stifled a grin at the thought of Jay's expression should he ever be presented with these tokens of her daughter's regard. She knew enough about him to know that he would eat the proffered gift whether he wanted it or not, but as yet Lucy's enthusiasm for the task of baking far outweighed her skill.

An hour later, both girls raincoated and welling-toned against the heavy rain that had started to fall, they set out for Whitegates.

As Claire opened the front door, the wind shipped it from her fingers, shrieking malevolently and making her gasp for breath. Both little girls clung firmly to her hands as they hurried down the deserted village street. Luckily the wind was behind them, otherwise Claire wasn't sure how they would have managed to walk. It had increased tremen-dously in velocity since she had fetched them home from school, and the heavy, rain-sodden clouds darkening the sky promised a very unpleasant night. Already there was evidence of the storm's havoc in the branches that had fallen from some of the trees, reminding Claire that she would have to find someone to prune her own fruit trees.

Icy flurries of rain stung their faces; the girls' hooded coats kept them fairly dry, but Claire's raincoat had no hood, and one look at the weather had convinced her of the folly of trying to use her umbrella. She could feel the rain soaking into her hair, releasing its errant curl, and the walk down the country lane to Whitegates, which was normally such a pleasure, had become more of an ordeal.

The house was warm, thanks to Claire's foresight in turning on the central heating when she had called earlier with the shopping. She made both girls strip off their wellingtons and coats in the kitchen, hanging them up to dry.

Jay's flight should have landed by now, but the bad weather might have delayed it. She glanced at her watch and frowned. It was barely five o'clock, but already it was very dark outside.

Having checked that both girls had put on their slippers, she agreed that they could go into the sitting-room to watch television.

Despite the expensive furnishings, the house always struck Claire as being very unwelcoming. She had always been very sensitive to atmosphere, and it sometimes seemed to her that the house was rejecting its inhabitants in the same way that a child will reject those it senses do not give it love.

The kitchen was fitted with every electrical device known to man, or so it seemed; the units were undoubtedly very expensive and stylish, but Claire found the white and grey décor of the room distinctly chilling. It was not a kitchen she could ever imagine herself enjoying working in. It was too glossy and sterile, looking more like something out of a magazine advertisement than part of a home. She always felt faintly uncomfortable in it, afraid almost of leaving so much as a fingermark on the brilliant work-tops.

What she had seen of the rest of the house was the same: sterile and cold. She often wondered who had chosen the décor, Jay or his wife. It seemed inconceivable that any woman with a small child would opt for off-white carpet and white leather furniture, but then neither could she see Jay choosing the thick white goatskin rugs in the drawing room.

White was the colour of purity; it was also the colour of snow, and that was how Claire perceived the house's décor, cold and frigid, unwelcoming, and unliveable-in.

She turned on the oven and took out of the fridge the casserole she had brought with her earlier in the day. She didn't normally prepare a meal for Jay, but tonight was an exception; no doubt he would be feeling both cold and tired when he did arrive.

Both she and the girls had eaten at the cottage. She didn't like the thought of them spilling anything on that sterile white marble kitchen table, or those immaculate grey tiles that covered the floor.

Jay had managed to find an agency who had agreed to take over the cleaning of the house, but as yet he had found no one who could care for his daughter. Secretly Claire was glad, and she knew that when the time eventually came she would miss Heather very much indeed. Lucy, with her sunny practical nature, was not the slightest bit jealous or resentful about sharing her mother with her friend.

As she moved automatically about the kitchen she frowned, wondering what the future held for Heather: a succession of nannies, perhaps, followed by boarding school? There were doubtless many children for whom such a regime would lead to a perfectly happy and well adjusted adult life, but Heather was so sensitive and withdrawn already. It was none of her business what arrangements Jay might choose to make for his daughter, Claire reminded herself firmly, but no amount of logic or reason could cancel out the bond of love that had built up between Heather and herself. When she lost her, it would in some ways be like losing her own child. Ridiculously, especially in the circumstances, she was already worrying about whether someone else would know how much care and cherishing the little girl needed. And that wasn't her only concern. She was also worried that Heather would see her withdrawal from her life in the manner of a betrayal, or worse, and although she had scrupulously tried to prepare her for their eventual parting, she sensed that Heather was too young to genuinely comprehend what lay ahead.

It was gone seven o'clock when Claire eventually heard Jay's car draw up outside.

Lucy came dashing into the kitchen almost before the engine had died.

'Jay's back!' she called out excitedly, pouting a little when Claire grasped her firmly by one arm and reminded her,

'Jay is *Heather's* daddy, Lucy.'

But for all her encouragement, Heather made no attempt to rush to the door and give Jay the exuberant welcome Lucy always favoured him with.

Claire saw the moment that the kitchen door opened that he was tired. He dumped his overnight case by the door and grimaced faintly across the kitchen.

'Sorry I'm late, but the plane was delayed.'

'Yes, we thought it might be.' She gave Heather a little push towards her father, releasing a faintly tense breath as the little girl gave him a slightly shy hug.

Lucy had no such inhibitions, flinging herself against his knees and lifting up a shining little face for his kiss.

With one little girl in his arms and the other clinging to his side, he still managed to retain the

aura of the male predator rather than that of
domesticity.

His hair had grown, Claire noticed idly, and he
seemed to have lost a little more weight. It was
stupid and totally unnecessary for her to worry
about him; if he knew, he was more likely to be
irritated by her concern than anything else.

'Something smells good.'

'It's a casserole. I thought you might be hungry.'

'I am. Have I got time to shower and change?'
Claire nodded her head.

'Good. How about someone bringing me a
drink?' he suggested, putting Heather down and
smiling at her.

'I'll do it,' Lucy piped up instantly, and Claire
suppressed a faint sigh.

'Why don't both of you do it?' suggested Jay
diplomatically. 'I shan't be long,' he promised
Claire. 'About ten minutes.'

Of course she was the one who poured out the
whisky and soda she knew he liked, warning
Heather to be careful as she carried it upstairs. She
knew which was Jay's room, but she had never been
inside it; there was no need. And yet as she stood at
the bottom of the stairs watching her charges'
careful progress she had an instant's appalling
awareness of Jay's lean body as he divested it of the
civilisation of clothes.

She shuddered tensely, closing her eyes to blot out
the image, and when she opened them again she
was trembling violently. She had never seen a
naked man, not really, and she had never wanted to,
so why that brief, illuminating image?

Jay was as good as his word, returning downstairs

within ten minutes, dressed in jeans and a checked wool shirt. His hair was still damp, and the clean male scent of his soap mingled with the aroma of the casserole, cutting sharply through the domestic atmosphere of the kitchen, bringing in an alien and predatory note that made Claire's body tense as she moved automatically away from him.

She saw him frown, his mouth tightening as though in some way her reaction displeased him.

'You should know by now that I'm not going to pounce on you, Claire.'

Her face flushed. 'I know that.'

'Then why the so-obvious retreat?'

'Perhaps I'm just one of those people who likes a lot of personal space.'

'Maybe, but you must have allowed it to be invaded at one time,' he retorted, glancing meaningfully at Lucy, just in case she should be unaware of what he was saying.

Claire gnawed nervously at her bottom lip, wondering what on earth she could say, but to her surprise, Jay made a sound of wry self-disgust and apologised quietly,

'I'm sorry. It's been a hell of a fortnight, and the delay in landing didn't help matters. That doesn't excuse me taking my frustrations out on you, I know. It's good to come home and find you here, Claire,' he added slowly, totally confounding her.

'I . . . we really ought to be leaving.' She placed his meal in front of him, avoiding his eyes. 'It's getting late . . .'

'You're not walking back on a night like this. I'll run you there after I've eaten.'

To drag him out again on a night like tonight,

when he was plainly so tired, was the last thing Claire wanted, but she sensed that to argue would only harden his determination.

'I'll make you some coffee,' she suggested instead.

'You know, delicious though this is, it's a little bit off-putting to eat it all alone. Next time, why don't we all eat together?'

Taken thoroughly off guard by his statement, Claire stared at him. She had scrupulously avoided doing anything that might even hint at any degree of intimacy between them, and for him to suggest that they all ate together, almost as though they were a family unit . . .

To save herself from pursuing her thoughts any further she said quickly, 'I don't like letting the girls eat in here. Everything's so spotless,' she told him, seeing his uncomprehending frown. 'I'm always afraid they'll make a mess.'

She saw his attention focus on the kitchen and sweep round it, as though he were seeing it properly for the first time.

'Susie was responsible for all the decorating and the furniture.'

'It's very sophisticated and luxurious,' Claire hurried to say, hating the thought of him thinking she was criticising his ex-wife, 'but . . .'

'But it's also sterile and clinical,' he supplied for her in a clipped voice, surprising her with his perception. 'Unlike your cottage, it isn't a home, is it?'

She bit her lip, unable to look at him.

'It's the woman who makes a place a home, not the furnishings . . .'

He pushed his plate away suddenly, and Claire wondered if he was thinking of his ex-wife. Despite his claim that he no longer loved her, did he perhaps miss her more than he allowed anyone to know?

It was just gone eight o'clock when Jay drove away from Whitegates. The two girls were in the back of the car, Claire sitting in the front next to him.

She thought as they drove down the village street that there seemed to be a good deal more activity than was usual, but it was only when they turned the corner that Claire saw why, and then all she could do was to sit motionless in shock and stare out of the car window.

One of the huge elms had lost a heavy main branch during the storm. It had crashed across the road and smashed down on the house opposite—her house, Claire acknowledged in shocked comprehension. She couldn't speak; she couldn't do anything but lift appalled eyes to Jay's grim face. Why was he looking like that? An expression of shocked disbelief in his eyes that was surely far too intense, bearing in mind the very casual nature of their acquaintanceship. And then it hit her— Heather could have been in there with Lucy and herself; Heather could have been asleep in that front bedroom where she could now see a gaping hole in the wall.

'I . . .' Hardly aware of what she was doing, Claire struggled to open the car door. A crowd of people were standing outside the house staring up at it.

'You stay here.' Jay's hand on her arm held her rigid in her seat, his voice unusually harsh. 'I'll deal with it. You look after the girls.'

She wanted to protest that it wasn't his problem, that somehow she would cope alone as she had coped with so many other things, but she wasn't given the opportunity to say anything. He was out of the car and shouldering his way through the massed crowd before she could open her mouth.

He was only gone for ten minutes. Claire could see him in conversation with another man. Both of them glanced up at the house from time to time as they spoke.

Slowly the reality of what had happened was seeping into her. That was *her* home with the gaping holes in the roof and front wall where the heavy branch had crashed through. Her house ... her home ... She started to shake with shock; silly, really unimportant things, such as the fact that she had only just done the ironing and everything would now need washing again, preventing her from taking in the full enormity of what had happened.

It took Lucy's anxious, 'Mummy ... where are we going to live?' to alert her to it, and then she could think of no answer to give her daughter. Her thoughts ran round and round in frantic circles as she tried to grapple with the shock of what had happened. Perhaps Mrs Vickers would put them up. Thank God they hadn't been inside when the branch had fallen ...

Jay came back and slid into the car beside her.

Claire struggled with her seat belt.

'I must go and ask Mrs Vickers if we can stay the night with her. I ... I must go inside and find our clothes, I ...'

'For God's sake, you're not going anywhere. The

house is unsafe!' Jay told her grimly, his voice so angry that she actually focused her eyes on him, unaware of how vulnerable and young she looked in her jeans and sweater, her hair curling wildly round her small face.

'I've just been talking to someone from the council. He says the house is unsafe. You can't go back inside.'

'But our clothes. My . . .'

'Damn your clothes!'

She hadn't heard him swear before, and the violence in his voice shocked her. In the darkness of the car her eyes widened, her body shaking suddenly with the drenching onset of reality.

'You're coming back with me,' Jay told her flatly. 'There's plenty of room at Whitegates.'

'Mrs Vickers . . .'

'For God's sake, Claire!' he exploded tensely. 'Why are you always so damned independent? You hate me doing the slightest thing for you. You didn't even want me to run you home tonight, did you? Did you?'

How could she explain to him that she hated being reliant on anyone? Suddenly it all seemed too much; she could feel the tremors of reaction building up inside her. She wanted to cry, but she couldn't let herself, not in front of Jay and the girls.

'You've done me enough favours,' he reminded her grimly. 'Surely I'm allowed to do you one small one in return? You and Lucy will stay at Whitegates tonight, and every night until your own home has been repaired.'

'That could take weeks,' protested Claire, her

eyes darkening bleakly as she looked back at her small house.

'The council are going to put some men in to make sure it's safe; when they have we can come back down and collect your things. You realise that the council won't pay for the repairs, don't you, even though the tree is on council-owned land?'

She hadn't thought that far ahead yet, and she looked at him blankly. Her mind seemed to be working very slowly.

'But surely my own insurance . . .'

For some reason Jay's mouth compressed grimly.

'Maybe,' he agreed at last, 'but most insurance companies class something like this as an "Act of God".'

When he saw that she was looking uncomprehendingly at him, he explained tersely,

'It isn't one of the risks they cover—they won't pay out under the policy. You'll have to find the money for the repairs yourself.'

Claire had too much pride to let him see what she was feeling. She turned her face away, so that he wouldn't see her shock. If the insurance company wouldn't pay out, what on earth was she going to do? How could she possibly afford to pay for the restoration work herself? A terrible, icy sense of fear engulfed her. A vision of the cramped council flat she and Lucy had lived in before they moved to the cottage rose up in front of her and wouldn't go away. She couldn't go back to that, not now that she had had a taste of the pleasure that life could be in attractive surroundings. Fate couldn't be so cruel, surely?

Jay had set the car in motion, but she was barely

aware of it. If only tomorrow wasn't a Saturday. It would be Monday before she could get in touch with the insurance company, before she would know where she stood. Surely Jay was wrong? The house must be covered for this kind of accidental damage.

Round and round her thoughts went in a feverish dance that took her no further forward and did nothing to alleviate the horrendous sense of oppression hanging over her.

CHAPTER FOUR

'I EXPECT you'll want to go down to the village and look at the cottage. I'll run you down there if you like.'

All four of them were having breakfast in the grey and white kitchen, which now looked lamentably untidy.

Claire had barely slept at all last night and breakfast was the very last thing she had wanted, but nothing seemed to impair Lucy's appetite, and she owed it to Jay to at least make some attempt to repay his hospitality. And anyway, it helped to keep busy.

'There's no need. I don't mind walking.'

'No, I'm sure you don't,' Jay's voice was dry, 'but you're going to want to collect some clothes for yourself and Lucy, and you can hardly carry them back with you.'

She wanted to protest that there was no need for him to involve himself in her affairs in this way, but the words stuck in her throat. She still couldn't totally comprehend what had happened. Last night in the bustle of making up beds for herself and Lucy, and getting both girls settled for the night, there hadn't been time to dwell on what had happened. Later, alone in bed, in the austere off-white bedroom Jay had suggested she use, there had been too much time, too many worries crowding into her mind for her to be able to sort things out into any sort of order.

As she sipped her coffee she stared out of the kitchen window. The sky was a perfect pale blue, the sun palely gold; last night's gale had died out and it was hard to look at the beautiful perfection of the crisp autumn day outside and remember what last night had been. Part of her stubbornly wanted to pretend that it hadn't happened at all.

'Mummy, can we go and play outside?'

Nothing seemed to daunt Lucy. This morning her daughter was her normal cheerful self, but Lucy didn't realise, as she did, exactly what effect that falling branch was likely to have on her life. Every time she thought about the future she could feel the panicky, helpless feeling swirl through her. She put down her coffee, knowing that her hand was trembling.

'Yes, yes, but put your wellingtons on, and no going outside the garden.'

Her response was automatic, her eyes barely even focusing on the two small jean-clad figures as they opened the back door.

As soon as they had gone she stood up. The intimacy of the kitchen with only Jay and herself in it made her feel uncomfortable. 'I . . .'

'Sit down.'

His voice was harsh, and she obeyed it automatically, looking at him with shocked, bewildered eyes as he poured her a fresh cup of coffee and brought it over to her.

'You've had a bad shock,' he told her curtly, 'and you're feeling the effects of it. It happens to all of us at times.'

'I'm all right.' Her lips pressed tightly together,

panic surging through her at the thought that he was aware of her weakness.

'For God's sake, what is it about you that won't allow you to turn to anyone for help? Independence is fine, Claire, but there is such a thing as taking it to extremes, or is it just *me*? Is it the thought of *me* helping you that makes you react like this?'

'I . . .' Her throat seemed to have seized up. She swallowed and managed to say painfully, 'I don't like being beholden to anyone.'

'I don't believe I'm hearing this! Beholden? It's positively Biblical! I'm the one who's *beholden* to you, Claire, not the other way round. When I brought you back here last night, I felt as though I were dragging you here against your will; every time I come within arm's length of you, you cringe away as though you think I'm about to commit rape!'

He stopped when he saw her face. Coming on top of everything else it was too much. She started to shake so violently that she spilled her coffee.

'What is it? What did I say?'

Jay took the cup from her, careful not to get too close to her, but she was barely aware of him.

'Claire, what is it? Surely you don't think I'd hurt you in some way, do you?'

She shook her head.

'Then what is it?' He frowned. 'Lucy's father?' His eyes narrowed. 'Is it your husband, did he . . .'

She felt the bubble of hysterical laughter well up inside her like a painful lump.

'There was no husband . . . I was never married . . . Lucy . . . I was raped on my way home from school when I was eighteen. My parents had just

died . . . I was still living in the house. I never saw
his face; he came up behind me and knocked me
out. When I came round I was in his car. I tried to
stop him, but he . . .' She shuddered tensely, trying
to stop the memories coming back. 'Afterwards he
pushed me out of the car and drove off . . .'

'Oh my God! The police?'

'I never told them. I couldn't tell anyone. Only the
doctor when I realised I was pregnant . . .'

'I would never have guessed. You love Lucy so
much.'

'I didn't know if I would, not until she was born.
But it wasn't her fault.'

'And that's why you don't want a husband, is it,
Claire—because of what happened?'

'I don't like men coming anywhere near me. I
don't want any sort of intimate relationship with
them. I can't explain it, I . . .' Claire shook her
head, trying to dispel her disturbing memories.

'You don't need to,' Jay told her curtly. 'I'm not
totally devoid of imagination.'

'I don't think I can bear it if I lose the cottage.
Before we came here Lucy and I had a council
flat . . .' She shuddered again, suddenly feeling
intensely cold. What on earth had prompted her to
break down like that? She had never, ever confided
to anyone other than her doctor the true circumstances surrounding Lucy's conception. She had
never wanted to tell anyone before. The events of
that night were something she thought she had
locked safely away.

It was the shock of what had happened to the
cottage, of course; but that didn't mitigate her sense
of self-betrayal.

'I shouldn't have told you,' she muttered, trying to stand up. 'I . . .'

'You hate revealing anything of yourself to others, don't you, Claire? Well, I can sympathise with that.' Jay stood up too, reaching out to steady her as she trembled. 'It's a fault I think I share, but I had hoped that you and I were becoming friends. Friends trust one another; I want you to feel that you can trust me. You think that what you've just told me makes you vulnerable to me,' he added, watching the give-away expression on her face. 'But I've been equally vulnerable to you—more so, possibly, and your strength and kindness when Heather was missing are something I will never forget, and never be able to repay,' he added quietly. 'Now go upstairs and get your coat, and then we'll drive down to the village and see what the situation is with the cottage. Oh, and Claire,' he added, as she headed for the door, 'I want you to know that you and Lucy can stay here for just as long as it takes to get things sorted out, and before you say a word, it won't be all one-sided. While you're living here, I'm getting a housekeeper and a nanny for Heather all rolled into one.'

She couldn't dispute the truth of what he said, but his other comment—that they could be friends, that they were equally vulnerable to one another—how true were they?

As she went upstairs she felt curiously empty, as though by telling him about Lucy she had somehow lost a part of herself. Why *had* she told him? To make him angry? To shock him? To gain his pity? She didn't know the reason.

She wasn't gone very long, and when she came

back down she opened the kitchen door so quietly that it was several seconds before he realised she was back. He was standing in front of the window and she could see his expression quite clearly. There was a bleakness about his mouth that made something deep inside her ache, and then he saw her, and his expression changed, the bleakness hidden away.

'Ready? Come on, then. We'll collect the girls on our way.'

Not even the sparkling perfection of the blue and gold autumn day could alleviate the stunning shock of seeing the cottage by daylight.

Darkness had somehow softened the reality of the carnage the falling branch had caused, but now, in the bright sunshine, nothing could disguise the huge hole in the roof, or the smaller one in the front wall. A pile of shattered roof slates lay in the front garden, the whir of saws as council workers busied themselves clearing as much of the mess as they could blurring into a dull, numbing sound as Claire stared helplessly at her home.

'Wait here a moment.' For once she didn't move away as Jay touched her arm. 'I'll check to find out if it's okay to go inside.'

It was too much of an effort to protest that he had no need to do these things for her—that she was perfectly capable of doing them herself. Instead she simply stood numbly where he had left her. Mrs Vickers came out of her house.

'Thank goodness you weren't here!' The old lady shook her head. 'My daughter came round last night after it happened. She wanted me to go home with her, but I wouldn't. I've lived here all my life and

I'm not moving out now,'

Jay came back. 'It's safe to go inside, just as long as we're careful. I'll come with you.'

Something strange had happened to Claire. She felt too numb to object to his assumption of control. Mrs Vickers offered to keep an eye on Lucy and Heather, and so, trying to conceal her inner trembling, Claire followed Jay into the house.

A film of dust covered everything, particles of it still swirling in the air, making her gasp for breath.

On the far side of the room was the small desk where she kept all her important papers. Her insurance policy was in it, and yet she found herself reluctant to move towards it.

'You'll need enough clothes to last you for quite some time. Pack as much as you can,' Jay told her. 'I'll wait down here for you. Just give me a shout if you need help.'

Even in the midst of her shocked anguish Claire recognised his awareness of her need to be alone. She wanted to thank him, but somehow the words just wouldn't come.

Her suitcases had once belonged to her parents. They were old and battered, and she filled them automatically, emptying drawers. Luckily most of Lucy's clothes were stored in her own room.

Lucy's room. Like a sleepwalker she dropped the pile of underwear she was putting in the case and walked slowly towards the other bedroom. The door was slightly open; she pushed it and walked in.

The two small beds were broken, crushed beneath the weight of the heavy branch. Dust and debris covered the once immaculate duvets that she had made with such love and care. Half a dozen or so slates had fallen through the roof and ceiling on to the beds.

She must have made a sound without being aware of it, because just as the full horror of what might have happened struck her and her body started to convulse in shocked waves of reaction Jay pushed open the bedroom door.

She had a fleeting glimpse of that same bleak expression on his face, intensified this time, and then she was in his arms, her face pressed against his shoulder.

'Come on—it's all right. They're both safe, Claire. Nothing happened.'

She wasn't aware of him as a man in those moments as she let her body absorb the strength of his; he was just someone who shared and understood her anguish.

'But it could have done. I knew the roof needed attention. I ... If something had happened, it would have been my fault!'

Hysteria built up inside her. She started to cry, hard, gulping sobs that tore painfully at her chest. She hadn't cried for years, not since her parents died, but there had been no one to comfort her then, no Jay to hold her in his arms and tell her that everything was all right.

'If you hadn't been coming home this weekend! If ...'

'Stop it! I know what you're going through. Do you think I didn't go through hell myself when Heather went missing; do you think I didn't hate and blame myself? Come on. Finish packing your things and then we'll go.'

Suddenly she felt acutely self-conscious, and her

body tensed within the protective circle of his arms. As though he sensed her feelings he released her immediately stepping back from her.

As he turned away he added casually, 'If you know where your insurance policy is it might be a good idea to collect that as well. I could get my broker to have a look at it for you if you like. Sometimes they're in a better position to bring pressure to bear than we mere individuals.'

He was being tactful, Claire knew, giving her time to recover herself. This emotional side of her nature was something she had held rigorously in check since the death of her parents, and the trauma of being raped and then discovering that she was pregnant had forced her to become even more self-sufficient. She and Jay shared that need to protect themselves from being hurt, she recognised as she finished her packing; in many ways they were alike, each sensing within the other a deep-rooted fear, hers of physical intimacy, his of emotional intimacy.

He was waiting for her when she went back downstairs. 'Okay now?'

She nodded her head. 'Yes, I'm fine. Fate seems to be smiling on the pair of us recently,' she added wryly. 'If you can call losing the roof over your head that.'

'Well, they say good things go in threes.'

Claire grimaced. 'I can hardly wait.'

An odd expression that she couldn't define crossed his face. What was he thinking about? His ex-wife? What business of hers was it if he was?

*   *   *

'So you don't think the insurance company will pay up?'

They were sitting in Whitegates' elegant, but to Claire's eyes sterile, drawing-room. Lucy and Heather were upstairs in bed, and she and Jay had just gone over her insurance policy.

Her heart sank as he shook his head gravely. 'I don't think so, but of course, I'll get my broker to check.'

Claire shivered, hugging her arms round her slim body. Without any money from the insurance company, how on earth was she going to pay for the damage to be put right?

'Of course, you know that you and Lucy are welcome to stay here for just as long as is necessary.'

It was a kind offer, but she didn't feel at all at home in this elegant, sophisticated house. She was terrified that Lucy might break something or leave muddy footprints on the off-white carpet. No wonder Heather was considerably less exuberant than her own daughter!

'I have to go back to Dallas on Wednesday. I'll give my broker a ring first thing Monday morning and see what he can sort out.'

Claire immediately felt guilty. 'You've got enough problems of your own without taking on mine as well.'

'It's no problem . . . and I owe you a few favours.'

'How long will you be away this time?'

'Only a few days. I'm hoping to get a final signature on a very large contract.'

Claire knew now that Jay's firm created reproduction Adam-style mouldings and Tudor-style panelled interiors, replicas in every detail of those made by master craftsmen in the past. There was a booming market for his products in America, especially in Texas, where they were enjoying a vogue, but the partner who had left the firm when he married Jay's ex-wife had been the salesman of the team, and Claire knew that Jay was now looking for someone to take his place—preferably an American with an entrée into the sort of society where the company's products found their best market.

'Once that's organised I can get down to doing some interviewing. I need an American based rep, then I can concentrate on the manufacturing side of the business over here.'

'Have you thought of setting up a factory in the States?'

'Yes, but it wouldn't work as well. The fact that our products are British gives them an added cachet. We're not just selling Adam-style décor, or Elizabethan libraries, we're selling something our customers can boast about to their friends.'

It was pleasantly relaxing sitting here with him like this. Claire found him fascinating to listen to and was genuinely interested in the way he had built up his business, so that when he said casually, 'Claire, I want to talk to you . . . about . . . about the man who raped you,' she was taken completely off guard.

'No, don't run away.' His fingers curled round her wrist, holding her in her chair as she tried to stand up. 'I'm not prying or asking out of any prurient curiosity. I just think it would help you to talk about it.'

'Therapy, you mean? Thanks, but no thanks. I

don't want to talk about it.' She tried to pull away but did not succesd.

'Have you ever tried?'

How could she? There had never been anyone to talk to about it. Her parents had been killed; her shock and horror after it had happened had been so great that she had simply gone home and shut herself in her bedroom for days, not eating, not sleeping, not doing anything. And then afterwards, when the reality of it had sunk into her, she had been too . . . Too what? Ashamed? Yes, there had been a sense of shame and of guilt, although why she had no idea. She had done nothing to encourage the man, nothing at all. He had physically abducted her, raped her and then thrown her out of his car like a used doll.

'I haven't pried into your private life, Jay, and I . . .'

'I'm not prying. Before you were raped, had you had any sexual experience at all?'

Claire's shudder gave her away, and this time when she stood up he stood too.

'I don't have to stay here and listen to this, Jay.'

'No, you don't, but one day you're going to have a teenage daughter who's going to want to talk to you about sex. How are you going to cope with that, Claire? Do you want her to inherit your inhibitions and fears?'

She swallowed hard. How on earth had he known how much that very dread haunted her: that she would infect Lucy with her own sickness?

'What is it about what happened that you find hardest to come to terms with?'

'My own guilt.'

The words were out before she could stop them, an expression of anguished despair flooding her eyes as she realised what she had said.

'You don't have anything to feel guilty about. You know that.'

Rationally perhaps she did, but emotionally . . .

'And because of that sense of guilt you've refused to allow yourself to feel any emotion for any other man—is that it?'

It was part of it; the major part, perhaps.

'You're a young and very attractive woman; haven't you ever wondered——'

'No.'

Her sharp denial cut across what he had been going to say.

'I wasn't about to make you a proposition,' he said grimly.

Claire looked at him. 'No, I know that. It's just that I can't even talk about the intimacy of a physical relationship with someone without remembering *him*.'

'Because what he did to you patterned your sexual responses,' Jay told her quietly. 'Claire, there's something I want to talk to you about.'

What on earth was he going to say? She watched as he walked over to a cupboard and poured them both a brandy.

She took a sip when he handed her the glass, feeling the raw spirit slide down her throat.

'When I said I wasn't going to proposition you, I meant it, but I do have a proposal to put to you. Neither of us, for differing reasons, wants the intimacy of a marriage based on the current concept of what marriage should be—neither of us want the physical or emotional commitment such a marriage involves. But there are other types of marriages: marriage entered into between two people who have other things to offer one another. Recently I've been giving it a lot of thought, and I believe that you and I could make such a marriage work. No, listen to me,' he demanded, when she started to protest. 'I need someone to look after Heather, but whoever I found could never give her the love she's already getting from you. I admit that when I first realised how attached to you she was getting I resented it, but you can give her something I can't, and I can give you and Lucy something you can't—security financially. He paused. 'I'm not going to ask you to give me your answer now, but I want you to think about it while I'm away. I can promise you that sexually you'll never need to fear anything from me.'

Claire stared at him. He didn't strike her as a man who lived like a monk, and as though he had read her mind, he said sardonically, 'I had an extremely satisfying sexual relationship with Susie, Claire, if that's what you're wondering, and if I want sex there are plenty of women who will oblige me. You needn't worry that I might embarrass you by indulging in a series of affairs, either; I won't.'

No, he wouldn't do that. All those overseas trips would no doubt provide more than adequate opportunities for relieving any sexual frustration he might experience.

'I don't know what to say . . .'

She knew what she ought to be saying if she'd any sense. She ought to be telling him that what he was suggesting was unthinkable.

'I don't want you to say anything right now. I

want you to think about what I've said, that's all.'

'If . . . if I agreed. Would we . . . would we live here?'

Now what on earth had made her ask that? It made it sound as though she was seriously considering his outrageous proposal.

'Yes.' Jay frowned. 'Don't you like the house?'

'It's very lovely, but I have nightmares every time the girls come in with muddy boots on.'

'Oh, that!' Instantly his face cleared. 'Yes, it is rather impractical. Susie chose the décor; someone once told her that white was her colour. Well, of course you can change it if you wish.'

It surprised Claire that he appeared so uninterested. In her experience, after the break-up of a relationship the partner who retained the house always either threw out everything connected with the relationship and started again, or clung desperately to every last thing that had been bought or chosen together; Jay fell into neither of those categories.

'Personally, I've never been all that keen on it,' he said. 'It looks lifeless.'

'You could always employ a nanny to take care of Heather, you know,' Claire felt bound to remind him.

'She loves you, and besides, a nanny couldn't give the same sort of permanence that would result from our marriage. Lucy needs a father just as much as Heather needs a mother, Claire. I like your daughter very much. I promise you I would always treat both of them equally.'

She knew that he would, and that he was right. Lucy was already becoming very attached to him.

On the face of it marriage between them would be the ideal solution to all their problems, but human beings were irrational creatures and marriage was such an irrevocable step—at least to her.

'Think about it,' said Jay, drinking the last of his brandy. 'I promise I won't mention it again until I come back from Dallas. That should give you time to weigh up the pros and cons.'

'But what if you should meet someone else . . . someone you could fall in love with . . .?'

His mouth compressed. 'I won't,' he told her starkly. 'I made that mistake with Susie and I soon learned that a woman only wants a man just as long as he remains out of reach. Once she knew I loved her that was it: she lost interest in me, emotionally if not sexually.'

He saw her expression and smiled grimly.

'Oh yes, there are women like that, Claire, women who enjoy sex uninhibitedly for sex's sake alone—and Susie was certainly one of them. She married me because she was expecting my child. She didn't want to, but I persuaded her. She thought I was a wealthy man; when she realised I wasn't, the marriage began to go sour, but even at its worst we still slept together, right up until the day she left with Brett. I learned after she'd gone that Brett hadn't been her only lover—he was just the richest. You see, his partnership with me was only one of his business interests. His father is a millionaire.'

He was still very bitter over the betrayal; Claire could see it so clearly. She could also see exactly why a marriage that was merely a business arrangement would appeal to him. But would he feel like that for ever? Might there not come a time when he was ready to love again, and when he did, what would happen to her?

Why was she even thinking about it? Surely a marriage between them was out of the question? But was it? Sitting talking to him tonight she had felt completely relaxed, and even happy, at least until he had brought up the subject of sex; she could live with him, she knew that, and more importantly, if she married him she would be bringing stability into the lives of both Lucy and Heather.

'Think about it, Claire,' he urged again.

CHAPTER FIVE

SUPPRESSING a faint sigh, Claire replaced the telephone receiver. The news from Jay's insurance broker, that the insurance company had no liability under her policy, had not come as a total surprise, but even so . . .

Pushing her depression to one side, she stood up and walked over to the drawing-room window. Through it she could see Lucy and Heather playing in the garden. A faint flush of excitement coloured Heather's pale skin, her happy laughter mingling with Lucy's.

'Let's have no illusions between us, Claire,' Jay had said before he left, when she had tried to point out to him that it went against everything she herself believed in for her to escape her financial problems by marrying him. 'We both have something the other needs. I know you well enough to know that you aren't the mercenary type, if that's what's worrying you.'

'But practical considerations alone are surely no secure base for something like marriage,' she had protested, and instantly his expression had hardened, his eyes shadowed and cold as he demanded in a clipped voice, 'What do you consider to be a sound base? Love? Is that what you want, to fall in love with someone and share your life and your body with him?'

She had sensed that he had been deliberately

reminding her of what marriage really was, and she had flinched away from him.

'I need you in my life, Claire, and I'm not too proud to tell you so,' he had continued. 'I need you as a mother for Heather, and perhaps later on, if you feel up to it, as a hostess for my business colleagues. If this contract with Dallas gets off the ground, several of the company's executives will be wanting to come over here and see how our operation works, but entertaining them isn't something I'd want to press on you if you felt you couldn't cope. I'm not ashamed to say that I need you, and if you're honest you need me too. We both know that you can't afford to have the cottage repaired. You don't want to go back to the sort of life you lived before you inherited it. I'm not buying you, Claire, and you're not selling yourself into marriage with me; we're entering a mutually beneficial arrangement.'

'You make it all sound very businesslike.'

'Isn't that what you want?' His expression had unsettled her. 'Or are you secretly looking for a Prince Charming to release you from your repression with the magic of his kiss?'

Her body tensed as she recalled the mockery in his voice as he delivered those words. Until that moment she had not even known herself how strong a hold that sort of foolish daydream had on her deepest and most private thoughts. Even so, she had denied it vigorously to him, and now, within a few short days he would be back, expecting an answer to the proposition he had put to her.

The girls' laughter reached her through the thick glass. Outside it was cold, frost riming the edges of the lawn where the sun had still not touched. Inside, the house was comfortably warm; pinching economies like needing to keep a check on central heating bills did not feature in Jay's world. Did she have the moral right to deprive Lucy of all that Jay could provide—and not just in the more obvious materialistic terms? There were other, more important considerations, such as the fact that already Lucy was becoming attached to Jay, that through him she could have the sort of education that would give her the very best sort of start in life, and that she and Jay together could give both girls the kind of stable, calm background that she sincerely believed gave untold benefits to the children who received them.

And it wasn't just her own child she had to consider. There was Heather as well. Heather, who was only just now starting to come out of her shell; Heather who clung to Claire at bedtime when she kissed her goodnight, who would appear at her side, almost out of nowhere, as if to check up on the fact that she was still there. All these considerations tipped the scales in favour of Jay's proposal.

And against it? What was there? Her own stubborn desire to remain self-supporting? Her dislike of any tag being attached to her that might label her as a mercenary, scheming woman taking advantage of a lone male with a small child to bring up? Her very deep-rooted fear of the state of marriage, of the powerful position in her life that it would give to Jay? But she already had his word that their marriage would be a business relationship only, and she knew that she could trust him. She had no illusions about Jay's sexuality. Even she could see that he was the sort of man whose passion was a powerful motivating force in his life—but he was also good-looking and male enough not to need to coerce any woman where sex was concerned.

Putting it at its most cynical and logical, what would be the point in him wasting his time trying to coax her into a sexual relationship when, doubtless, there were countless number of women only too eager to have that privilege? No, she had nothing to fear from him in that way.

But there were other dangers. Claire bit her lip, gnawing anxiously on it. She already knew how vulnerable she herself was to emotional bonding. Witness the way her feelings for Heather had grown to the point where her love for the little girl was almost enough on its own to make her accede to Jay's proposal.

Jay was a very charismatic and genuinely fascinating man. A man, moreover, who took the trouble to talk to her as an equal—a man whom it would be very easy to come to depend on, in a way she had not had someone to depend on since the death of her parents. Yes, there was a very real danger there, but surely the mere fact that she was aware of it would make her wary and careful. She would not burden Jay with an emotionalism he wouldn't want, even if it was only the emotion of friendship rather than sexual love.

Both of them, in their separate ways, had been crippled emotionally by life; both of them together could build a secure home for their children that would enable them to put down the strong roots every living thing needed to grow.

'When will Jay be back?'

'Later on this afternoon,' Claire responded.

'Can we go and meet him at the airport, please, Mummy?'

Claire shook her head firmly, ignoring Lucy's cry

of disappointment. As always, fortunately, her daughter's attention proved fairly easy to distract. She was unlike Heather in that respect, who would worry and brood over something until it was sorted out to her satisfaction.

Jay's return coincided with the half-term holidays. Claire had made tentative plans to take the girls to Bristol, mainly to buy them both new clothes, and she had also rashly promised a brief visit to the zoo.

How long would Jay wait before demanding an answer to his proposal? Not long, she suspected. He was a decisive man who would not tolerate shilly-shallying in others. Inwardly she knew that her decision had been made, but even so, actually telling Jay that she was prepared to marry him was something she wasn't looking forward to doing. Actually saying the words made it seem so final. She guessed that he wouldn't want to wait very long after her agreement before legally formalising their marriage.

Partly because Lucy had pleaded with her and partly to avoid being left alone with him, Claire had agreed that the girls' evening meal could be delayed so that they could share it with Jay.

She had no real idea or knowledge of his culinary preferences, but knowing the delays that could arise both during the flight and after it, she had made another casserole, a slightly more glamorous one this time: chicken breasts in a special sauce, which she intended to serve with duchesse potatoes, and fresh vegetables. She suspected that after several days in Dallas Jay would be heartily sick of prime steak, and so the chicken should be a welcome change.

Leaving both girls happily occupied in the kitchen with their crayoning books, she went upstairs to check on Jay's room.

Shortly after he had left she had entered it for the first time to strip his bed, and as it had then, when she opened the door and walked into it, its almost monastic austerity surprised her. She didn't know what she had expected, but it certainly hadn't been this coldly plain room, so empty of any personal possessions that it might have belonged to a hotel. The large bed was covered by a plain, dull spread. The bedside tables held only a telephone and an alarm clock. A bank of fitted wardrobes and cupboards presented a plain cream front to her cursory glance. Brown curtains hung at the window to tone with the neutral-coloured carpet.

All in all, the room was spectacularly uninspiring and, unlike the rest of the house, did not reveal the decorative hand of Jay's ex-wife.

Claire wondered why. She already knew from Heather which room had been her mother's, and although she had not as yet ventured inside it she had assumed that Jay must have shared it with her. She could well understand him choosing to sleep in a different room after the break-up of the marriage, but what she could't fathom out was why this one room out of the whole house had not been redecorated.

Arming herself with clean sheets, she set about making the bed. Jay had his own private bathroom off his bedroom, and she was just on her way out when she remembered he would need fresh towels.

The telephone rang, distracting her. She hurried to answer it, surprised to hear Jay's voice as she picked up the receiver.

'I just thought I'd let you know I'd landed. I'm calling in at the factory on my way back. I should be home for about six.'

He didn't say anything else. Claire had no opportunity to ask him about the contract. He had sounded tired, and he had made no mention of his proposal—but then he wouldn't, of course.

'What are we going to have for pudding?' Lucy asked her as she walked into the kitchen.

'You could make an apple pie,' suggested Heather eagerly. 'It's Daddy's favourite.'

Telling herself that it was what she had, after all, planned to make, Claire cleared the table and started making pastry, carefully checking the enthusiastic assistance of her two 'helpers'.

Baking was something she had always found therapeutic, and somehow one thing led to a other. The mouthwatering aroma of cooking pastry and fruit mingled with that of the chicken, and Claire was just putting a final dollop of mixture in to some bun tins when she heard the sound of a car.

'It's Jay,' shrieked Lucy eagerly, scrambling down from her stool, and rushing for the back door.

Jay reached it first, his eyebrows lifting slightly as he walked in.

'You're early?' For some reason Claire felt oddly shaky. He looked so alien standing in the kitchen, in his immaculate business suit and his crisp white shirt.

'Yes ... and we've been making your very favourite—apple pie,' Lucy announced.

A sudden awareness of pastry-sticky fingers and flour-smeared hands made Claire dart forward to pick Lucy up before she could inflict any damage on his immaculate suit, but Jay forestalled her, swinging Lucy up into his arms, so that she shrieked with delight.

'Jay, your suit . . .' She reached up automatically to brush off the floury marks left by Lucy's hands and then realised to her mortification that her own were equally floury.

'Stop fussing, it will clean.'

He put Lucy down and held out his arms to Heather. As always she clung to Claire's side. Bending down, she gave her a little push. 'Go and kiss Daddy hello.'

Over Heather's dark head Jay gave her a wry look.

'Odd, isn't it? *Your* daughter can't wait to fling herself into my arms, whereas mine . . .'

'Give her time,' Claire urged in a low voice. 'She's such a sensitive child, and she's had too many upheavals in her life. She needs to learn that she can trust you always to be there. She needs stability . . .'

'Yes, she does.'

The look he gave her was direct and determined, and ridiculously, Claire felt hot colour sting her face.

Lucy's impatient tug on her skirt caused a welcome diversion. 'Mummy, what's a woman?'

Claire was perplexed. She looked down at her daughter. 'I'm not sure what you mean, Lucy.'

'Well, when you were talking to Mrs Vickers after school yesterday and Heather and me went in the post office, Mrs Simmonds was there and she said that you were Lucy's daddy's woman.'

Over her daughter's auburn curls Claire's shocked eyes met the grim expression in Jay's.

'I . . .'

'It means that your mummy and I are going to get

married,' Jay announced, ignoring the choked
sound that emitted from Claire's throat.

'You mean like real mummies and daddies?'
Lucy was plainly ecstatic about the idea. 'And we'll
live here for always?'

'Something like that,' he agreed urbanely. He was
still watching her, Claire realised, a hard purpose-
fulness in his eyes that warned her that he had made
her decision for her, and he wasn't going to let her
back out of it.

She ought to have been furious with him for his
high-handedness, but in reality it was a relief. Her
decision had in fact already been made, but the
knowledge that their relationship was the subject of
village gossip and speculation wouldn't have made
it any easier for her to communicate it to Jay.

Feeling rather feeble, she said unsteadily, 'Lucy,
you're covered in flour; why don't you and Heather
go upstairs and clean up?'

As Jay put her down, Heather put her hand on
Claire's arm and looked up at her. 'Are you really
going to be here for always?'

The expression in her eyes wasn't something
Claire had the strength to withstand. Going down
on her heels so that her face was on a level with the
little girl's, she asked huskily, 'Is that what you
want, Heather, for me to be here for always?'

'Yes . . . yes . . .' A fierce hug accompanied the
emphatic words.

'Then I will be.'

Although she was speaking to Heather, Claire
knew that her words were meant for Jay. As she
stood up she looked at him and caught an
expression on his face that puzzled her. He looked
like a man who had been under almost unendurable

pressure and who had now found it relaxed.

Claire waited until both girls were out of the kitchen before speaking to him.

'You had no right to tell them that.'

He didn't argue with her, simply flexed his body as though it ached. 'It saves you from making any decision though, doesn't it?'

Claire's mouth compressed as she caught the tinge of contempt in his voice. Did he really think she was incapable of deciding for herself? On the verge of telling him that she had already decided to marry him for herself, she caught the words back, and said instead, 'I shouldn't have thought a little bit of village gossip would worry you to that extent.'

'It doesn't,' he agreed flatly. 'At least, not on my own behalf, and especially when there are no grounds for it—but I don't want either of the girls to be subjected to the sort of sniggered whispers that go the rounds of every school playground. Okay, right now they're too innocent to understand what's being said, but for how long?' He looked at her, and for the first time Claire saw the exhaustion in his face. 'Before we go any further, can I take it that since you didn't contradict what I said to the girls about our plans for the future, you are going to marry me?'

'It doesn't seem that I have much choice now, does it?' Claire responded tartly.

Almost instantly his face closed up, his mouth going hard. 'No, it doesn't, does it?' he agreed with more than a hint of acerbic grimness. 'And since that's settled, if you don't mind, I'd like to go upstairs and have a shower.'

Seeing the weariness in his tense back, Claire wished her own part in their exchange unsaid. The

problem was that she had been so shocked by
Lucy's innocent revelations that things had got out
of hand. She had had everything carefully
planned—a family meal over which she and Jay
could relax in one another's company, and then a
quiet evening with the girls, followed perhaps by a
chat together in front of the sitting-room fire, when
she would have felt relaxed enough to convey her
intentions to him. Now, abruptly, all her plans had
been swept away, and far from being relaxing, the
evening looked like being extremely tense indeed.

Still, looking at it from Jay's point of view, it had
hardly been a good homecoming. She could
remember how tired and tense her father used to be
after dealing with a difficult business meeting, and
Jay had had a whole series of them. It could hardly
have helped his frame of mind to be greeted by the
artless announcement, the moment he stepped
through the door, that the whole village was
gossiping about them.

She was just about to clear the kitchen table when
she suddenly remembered that she had forgotten to
put clean towels in Jay's room.

The airing cupboard was full of clean towels, and
she selected a pile at random, pausing outside his
bedroom door to knock.

She heard him call out, 'Come in,' and pushed
open the door with her hip.

'I just remembered that you don't have any
towels . . .' She froze, her voice locking in her throat
as she realised that she had interrupted him while
he was getting undressed.

He had discarded his suit jacket and his shirt.
The latter lay on the floor, a puddle of white cloth.
She stared at it for what seemed like a long time, as

she fought to control the rapid rise and fall of her chest.

She couldn't look at him again. One brief glance at that tough, muscle-hardened torso with its rough shadowing of hair had been enough to freeze her where she stood.

Obliquely she was somehow aware of her own body as though she had stepped outside it. She could feel the rapid pulse of her blood along her veins; she could hear the frightened thud of her heart. She knew that her eyes had dilated with the shock and that her breathing sounded raspy and painful.

The room was warm, and yet somehow she could feel the soft movement of air against her skin like an icy embrace, as Jay moved.

'It's all right, Claire, it's all right . . .' She knew that he was aware of what had happened to her and that logically there was nothing for her to fear, but while her mind could comprehend it, her body could not. She saw him reach past her for his shirt and tug it on. All the time he was talking soothingly to her, but she barely heard him. She couldn't comprehend anything other than the maleness of his body; that blocked everything else out. She shuddered as he fastened the buttons, remembering that dark arrowing of hair disappearing beneath his belt.

'Claire, it's all right.'

He stepped towards her, taking the towels from her numb arms and putting them down on the bed. 'It's all right.' His hands gripped her arms, and felt their clenched muscles. He started to massage them, easing the frozen tension out of her.

'I . . .' Somehow she managed to unlock her tongue, a tide of fierce heat enveloping her as she realised how stupidly she had behaved. She was shaking violently now, perspiration breaking out all over her skin. Where she had been cold, now she was hot.

'It's all right . . . don't try to say anything. Come and sit down for a moment.'

Numbly she let him lead her to the bed, and gently push her down on to it. Now, with the raw evidence of his maleness concealed from her, she was able to get herself back under control.

'Is it always like this . . .?'

'Always?' She looked blankly at him.

'Mine can't be the first naked male chest you've seen, Claire,' he reasoned, catching the train of her thoughts.

That was true, but the others had been sanitised by their surroundings: on television, on the beach . . . Never, ever in the intimate confines of a bedroom; never, ever so close to her that she had seen the faint stickiness of sweat dampening the silky chest hair, or been aware of the musky male scent of a man's body.

'I . . .'

'Mummy, I'm hungry . . . when are we going to eat . . .?'

'I'm hungry too.'

Lucy and Heather stood in the open doorway.

'Will you and Daddy both be sleeping in here when you're married?' Heather enquired innocently.

Above her Claire heard Jay catch his breath. 'No,' he said roughly.

'You and Mummy didn't sleep in the same bed either, did you?'

'No,' he agreed. 'Claire's like your mother. She wants her own bedroom.'

'Why do you want your own room?' Heather asked her.

Claire got up and walked towards the door.

'Because she likes her privacy,' Jay answered for her. His voice sounded unfamiliarly harsh, as though something had hurt his throat. It couldn't be anything to do with her. A reaction perhaps to the memories Heather had unwittingly stirred up by mentioning her mother?

In spite of everything, supper was a convivially relaxed meal, any conversation gaps left by the two adults more than compensated for by the excited chatter of the two girls.

'Can we tell everyone at school about you and Mummy getting married?' Lucy asked Jay.

'If you think they'd be interested.'

An announcement like that was bound to cause more gossip than it squashed, at least until they were actually married, Claire reflected as she cleared away their plates and got out the pie.

'Claire's made apple pie for you 'cos it's your favourite, Daddy,' Heather told her father with a beam. 'She made it specially because you were coming home.'

'Did she? That's very kind of her.'

Against her will Claire found herself turning to look at him. In a low voice that neither of the girls could hear, he said softly, 'I think I'm going to like coming home to a wife who makes apple pies especially for me.'

For some extraordinary reason Claire felt herself tremble. To compensate for it she said sharply, 'Didn't Heather's mother . . .'

'No . . . No, Susie wasn't much of a cook,' said

Jay sardonically. 'Her talents lay in other directions.'

Yes, and she knew what those were, despite those separate bedrooms. Her face grew hot as she thought about the likely outcome had his ex-wife happened to walk into his bedroom when he was half naked.

'What's wrong?' asked Jay.

'Nothing.' How on earth had he come to have such long thick lashes? she wondered absently, fighting to disentangle her glance from his. They looked so soft, so at odds with the harsh angles of his face.

'Mummy, may I have some pie?'

Hurriedly Claire turned towards her daughter.

Much to her surprise, Jay joined in the girls' bedtime preparations. Heather was much more relaxed with him now, she noticed as she briskly handed both girls clean nightdresses.

'Clean your teeth and then straight into bed.'

'And then will you come and read to us?'

That was Heather, the dreamer. Claire was reading *The Secret Garden* to them, reliving her own childhood pleasure in the magic of the book. Out of the corner of her eye she caught the expression on Jay's face.

'Not tonight, it's Daddy's turn,' she said firmly, not letting herself respond to Heather's agonised expression.

That brief awareness between them when she had sensed Jay's feeling of rejection had gone, but she had been aware of it, just as she was aware of his pain whenever Heather turned from him to her.

He was upstairs for a long time. Claire busied herself in the kitchen, knowing that when he came down they would have to talk, but reluctant to do so.

He came in quietly, but she was still aware of him. She turned to look at him and was struck by the air of exhaustion that clung to him.

'You look tired.'

'It's been a long week. Heather still seems to see me in the guise of some sort of ogre. I can't believe that Mrs Roberts alone is responsible.'

Claire didn't either, but she had to choose her words carefully. 'She's a very sensitive child; she hardly knows you. You've been away such a lot. From what she tells me she hasn't spent much time with either you or her mother . . .'

'No. And if you're trying to tell me that in those circumstances it's hardly surprising that she wants to reject me, I know it, but that still doesn't stop me from . . . Every time I reach out to her she retreats from me, but with you . . .'

'Some little girls do respond better to their own sex, especially at that age,' she soothed. 'I know how you feel, though,' she added in a low voice. 'I feel equally guilty when I see how enthusiastically Lucy goes to you. It had never even occurred to me that she might miss having a father, even though I was very close to mine.'

She heard Jay sigh.

'I'm sorry I forced your hand earlier on.' He leaned back against the wall tiredly, hands pushed into his pockets. The material strained across his thighs and her attention was concentrated like a fly trapped in honey on the strong play of muscles there. Desperately she wrenched it away.

'I had already decided to accept your proposal,' she told him huskily. 'I've been trying all week to convince myself that you're right and that we'd each be contributing equally to the marriage, but . . .'

'But you still haven't managed to do it?' He made
a small explosive sound in the back of his throat as
he levered himself off the wall and came towards
her.

'You know what your trouble is, don't you,
Claire? You're too damned proud! Do you honestly
think that money can actually compensate for all
the things you can give Heather that I can't? No!
When I walked in here tonight she actually smiled
at me. Do you know how long it's been since she did
that? Since I came back to this house and found
anything like a welcome, in fact? To walk in here
tonight after a week spent arguing over the final
details of the contract . . .' He made a brief gesture
that encompassed without words what he was
trying to say. 'Susie wasn't much of a homemaker.
She never wanted to get married. She was a model
when I met her, and she bitterly resented being
dragged down here and buried alive in the country,
as she called it. If I hadn't stopped her, she'd have
had Heather aborted. Sometimes I wondered if . . .'

'No . . . No, you mustn't think that!' Claire's
voice shook with anguish for him. Without even
thinking about it she reached out and touched his
arm lightly.

It was strange to feel his living flesh beneath the
fabric of his shirt and her fingertips lingered briefly
before she realised what he was and hurriedly
withdrew.

'Let's go and sit down,' he suggested. 'We've got a
lot to talk about.'

In the sitting-room he poured them both a drink.
Claire sat on the edge of her chair, nursing hers
tensely. Jay shivered slightly as he sat down.

'It feels cold in here.'

'The central heating's on, but I suppose it was much hotter in Dallas.'

'Mmm ... I suppose it was, although I never got beyond my air-conditioned hotel room, or an equally air-conditioned suite of offices.'

'But you got the contract. I wish I'd known; I could have made a special celebratory meal.'

There was a moment's odd silence that for some reason made her skin prickle warningly, and then Jay said in a husky voice, 'I wish you'd known too. I think I could quite easily get used to being spoiled by you, Claire ... This room is cold,' he added abruptly. 'I've never liked it. It's too cold and sterile. So is the whole house, come to think of it, but I was desperate to find somewhere at the time, and Susie was no help, complaining that she hated everything we saw.'

Claire longed to tell him that there was nothing wrong with the house and that it was the décor that was at fault, but instead she said tactfully, 'I was wondering if you would mind if I changed things a little after we're married, Jay. Oh, nothing too expensive. It's just ...'

'Make whatever changes you wish. And Claire ...' She looked at him. 'Don't worry about what it costs, provided you aren't intending a wholesale refurnishing exercise with antiques.'

'I was wondering about using some of the company's products,' Claire suggested cautiously. An idea had taken root in her mind, but she wasn't sure what Jay's reaction would be. 'You did say that we might have to entertain American executives from the Dallas company, and I was thinking some of the rooms here could be redecorated using some of your products, as a sort of . . .'

'Showcase!'

Jay had been lounging back, his head resting
against the cream leather of the settee, and now he
sat upright, his eyes alert.

'Yes, it's an excellent idea, but it would involve
you in a lot of extra work, Claire—workmen in and
out of the house, as well as taking care of the girls—
and I'd have to leave all the planning and design to
you as well. Initially, until the orders start moving
smoothly, I'll be fully occupied keeping tabs on
them.'

'I don't mind.' She didn't. She would welcome
anything that would change the house from its
present austere state to something a little more
homely.

'Well, if you're sure, I'll get you some of our
brochures and you can browse through them and
see if there's anything you can use. In fact, I'd like to
make the arrangements for the wedding and get it
over with as soon as possible. I was thinking we
could get married in Bath; if you like we could
spend a couple of days there and I could take you
round the factory.'

'It would be even better if you could organise it to
fit in with half-term,' Claire suggested. 'I have
promised to take the girls to Bristol Zoo—and they
both need new clothes . . .'

'Fine. I'll organise something. You're going to
need to do some shopping for yourself as well.'

It was lightly said, but even so, Claire flushed.
She knew that her clothes weren't glamorous—far
from it—but there had never been any money to
spare to spend on herself.

'I . . . I don't need anything, Jay,' she lied.

'Yes, you do,' he corrected evenly. 'Claire, if you're going to act as my hostess, you're going to have to dress the part. American women are very clothes-conscious, especially Dallas women, and believe me, if the men are coming over here, their wives are going to want to come with them. It might even be worthwhile looking into ways and means of keeping them occupied—you know the sort of thing: a tour of Bath, and a couple of stately homes. Afternoon tea in thatched cottage villages.'

Surprisingly, instead of feeling daunted by what he had outlined, Claire felt a surge of interested excitement. She had never had a career, never really worked in the sense of being employed, but she had done well at school, and knew that she had a lively intelligence. To take on the role Jay was outlining would be a challenge, and one she felt she could respond to. And he was right—clothes; the right sort of clothes, would be an important part of that role.

'If it's the fact that I'll be paying for your clothes that's worrying you, then don't let it,' he advised her. 'Believe me, Claire, if I had to pay for a full-time nanny for Heather, plus a cook and housekeeper of the high calibre that you are, plus a social secretary-cum-hostess, it would cost me far, far more than you're ever likely to spend on clothes.'

'Ah, but that's why you want to marry me, isn't it?' she said lightly. 'So that you don't have to do that . . .'

'Partly. But more important is the stability and permanence you're going to bring to Heather's life. It's just as well that Lucy is such a sunny-natured child. No problems there with any incipient jealousy, I hope?'

'No, none at all. Lucy is a very well-adjusted little girl, luckily; I often wonder ...'

'Who she gets it from?' he said evenly. 'It's not my affair, Claire, but what are you going to tell her when she's old enough to start asking questions?'

She took a steadying breath. 'I can't tell her the truth.'

He seemed to consider for a moment and then said, 'No, perhaps not. So what will you tell her?'

'That I loved her father. That he and I were at school together ... That he was an orphan ...' she bit her lip. 'I thought I could tell her that he was killed in ... in an accident ...'

'Thus effectively making sure she won't go looking for him or for anyone connected with him. Mmm, I suppose it could work.'

His question led to one that had been bothering her. Putting down her half-empty glass, she stood up and walked nervously towards the window, before turning to face him.

'Jay, what will you do if your ... if Heather's mother ever wants her back?'

'She won't.' His voice was harsh, corrosive almost. 'Susie made that more than clear. Besides, I took the precaution of getting her to sign an agreement giving me total responsibility for Heather. Do you honestly think I would allow a child as sensitive as Heather is to be torn apart between two parents?'

'If Susie changed her mind and decided that she wanted to ... to come back, you ...'

'I what? Wouldn't be able to resist her?' He laughed bitterly. 'Don't you believe it! Sexually she could still turn me on, I suppose, but emotionally— no ... that's all gone, and besides, she won't come back. She's got what she wanted, now that she's the wife of Brett Brassington the Third.'

There was no mistaking the cynical bitterness in his voice, and Claire's heart ached for him. It was impossible for her to comprehend the sort of relationship he had had with his ex-wife, and as though he knew it, he said savagely,

'Our marriage was never the sort of marriage you can visualise, Claire. I loved Susie, yes, but it was an obsessive physical love that didn't last much longer than the honeymoon. I married her because she was carrying my child which she had threatened to abort, and she married me because she was twenty-six years old, and for a model, that's old. She could never accept or understand the amount of time I had to give to the business. Sexually she knew all the tricks there are to know; she knew exactly how to make me ache, and she enjoyed making me beg. You heard Heather: we had separate rooms—Susie's idea not mine,' he added broodingly. She kept me dangling on a thread for so long that after a while I just lost interest. Things weren't going well with the business. I was tired of arguing with her; tired of being made to pay and beg for sex; something inside me just seemed to shut off.' He laughed derisively. 'She couldn't believe it; she thought I was trying a few tricks of my own . . .' He broke off when he saw the confused look Claire was giving him, and explained rawly, 'Too much strain overloads the system, Claire; I lost the ability to respond to her in any way at all. Once that happened I think we both knew the marriage was over, and I know I was never her only lover, not even in the early days when I genuinely thought she did care. I tried to keep the marriage going because of Heather, but it wasn't any good. And when Susie found out that I was able, to put it bluntly, to respond to other women in a way I could no longer respond to her, that was the end. Her pride couldn't take it.'

Jay was saying that he had been impotent? Claire stared at him, totally unable to comprehend such an eventuality; to her, he seemed such a physical man. Her eyes widened and she looked at him, unable to hide her thoughts.

'You don't believe me?' He laughed again, this time properly. 'Thanks for the vote of confidence, but believe me, it's true. Even now . . .' he shrugged powerful shoulders and said lazily, 'suffice it to say that you need never worry that any brief flings I might have will damage our marriage. It's too important to me for me to risk it in any way.'

She did believe him, but she also wondered how on earth he had ever confused the obvious physical infatuation he had for his ex-wife with love. His own description of his feelings had been so lacking in that emotion that Claire had been both shocked and saddened by the emotional paucity of their relationship.

'I . . . I think it's time I went to bed.'

He glanced at his watch. 'Mmm, me too. Oh, by the way . . . the cottage . . .'

'The insurance didn't cover the damage,' Claire told him baldly.

'No, I guessed that, but something will have to be done about it. Leave it with me, will you?'

CHAPTER SIX

'RIGHT everything's arranged. We get married on Thursday in Bath. I've booked us into a hotel for a couple of days—that should give us enough time to get the girls and you re-equipped and to do a little bit of sightseeing.' He put down the briefcase he had brought from the car and opened it, the fabric of his suit jacket stretching taut across his back. Perhaps it was because the only other man she had ever lived with had been her father that she was so constantly aware of, and caught off guard by, the essential maleness of him. Perhaps she had lived too long in the softer world of women, and it was that which made her so conscious of the hardness of his muscled body.

'Here you are; I brought these back for you to browse through.' He handed her a pile of glossy leaflets. 'We don't have a design department as such, but if you feel you want to engage an interior designer . . .'

Claire shook her head decisively. Whitegates was going to be her home, and besides, she was looking forward to the challenge of re-planning it herself.

'Well, just as long as you don't start worrying about keeping costs down,' Jay warned her. He grimaced faintly and looked round the kitchen. 'While you're at it, how about doing something in here . . . something . . .'

'Warmer?' Claire supplied dryly.

'Mmm. And Claire, don't forget you're going to need to adapt some of the bedrooms into guest suites, complete with *en suite* baths.'

Claire laughed. 'It sounds more like I'm going to be running a hotel than a home!'

'Mmm, talking of which . . . This is the hotel I've booked us into, in Bath. I've organised a suite with three bedrooms—the girls can share. It's just on the outskirts of the town and has its own leisure complex, complete with swimming pool. 'Can Lucy swim?'

'Yes. Can Heather?'

'Yes.'

News of their impending marriage had spread through the village grapevine faster than an epidemic in a slum, and Claire had got used to being stopped in the street and discreetly pumped for more information. Overall, she gained the impression that the village thoroughly approved.

'It is such a nice arrangement,' Mrs Vickers innocently told her. The village apparently did not approve of such modern things as 'living together', and she gathered that Jay's ex-wife had not been particularly popular. Indeed, no one seemed to know much about her at all, other than the fact that she had run off with another man, leaving her small daughter behind.

Naturally, both little girls were wildly excited, anticipating the dual treat of the wedding plus the visit to Bath. Jay proposed that they leave after breakfast on the Wednesday morning, which would give Claire plenty of time to get all her shopping done before the Thursday afternoon ceremony.

A backlog of work at the factory kept him late

there most evenings, although he always tried to get back in time to read the girls a story. Heather was slowly starting to relax with him, and once or twice Claire even thought she saw a glimmer of anticipation in the little girl's eyes when he walked through the back door. And Lucy was uninhibitedly in favour of the marriage. Jay was her hero, and she worshipped him with an unashamed adoration.

Already it was November. Christmas loomed on the horizon, and unless she wanted the house to be in a total state of uproar over the Christmas holiday she would have to get a move on with her plans for the house, Claire realised as she picked up the brochures Jay had brought for her.

After supper Jay disappeared into his study, and Claire curled up on the leather couch, her feet tucked up underneath her as she browsed through the leaflets. There was a range of Victorian reproduction sanitaryware, which she thought was bound to impress the Americans, and she put the details on one side, turning to concentrate on the photographs of various types of reproduction plasterwork.

The large drawing room would lend itself very nicely to that sort of embellishment, and although not strictly Georgian, the house was old enough, the rooms high-ceilinged enough to take that sort of decorative detail. The thought struck her that she could probably get some sort of inspiration as to how to use the mouldings to best effect by studying photographs of original Adam-style rooms.

Jay had pointed out to her that although several firms manufactured similar products, they prided themselves on genuinely making an effort to reproduce even the finest detail of the original plasterwork, just as modern furniture makers were now using the original pattern books of men such as Chippendale and Hepplewhite, so that they could reproduce furniture which was comparable in quality and workmanship with the original. There was nothing either cheap or tacky about their products, Jay had told Claire, and the methods they used to make them reflected as far as possible the workmanship which had gone into the originals.

It seemed to Claire, as she studied the photographs of various mock room-settings, that both the drawing-room and dining-room could become showpieces for Jay's products, while the panelling could surely be an attractive addition to Jay's study?

As she worked through the literature, she made various notes, jotting down ideas that occurred to her for new colour schemes. Here in the sitting-room she had set her heart on a comfortable country house atmosphere with deeply cushioned settees in modern chintz, and colour-washed walls. A pretty, soft golden yellow perhaps . . . something warm and sunny. She wanted a room that people could be at leisure in. Somewhere where the girls could play, and Jay could relax.

She glanced at the clock, stunned to see that it was almost half past eleven. It was time she went to bed. She tidied up the papers, and then got up, yawning.

As she took her coffee cup to the kitchen she saw that there was still a light on in the study. On impulse she knocked briefly and opened the door.

Jay was sitting behind his desk, his tie loose and the top buttons of his shirt unfastened. His hair looked as though he had been pushing his fingers through it.

'Hello, still up?'

'Mmm. I got rather involved in my room planning. I'm going to bed now, though. Do you fancy a cup of coffee?'

'Yes, please. I've got quite a lot to do yet; I could do with something to keep me awake. Did you come to any conclusions—about how we could use our products?'

'Oh, yes, I've got loads of ideas . . . while we're in Bath I'll have to look round at fabric shops, that sort of thing. What is worrying me, though, is finding someone to install it properly.'

'Oh, we've got our own team to do that. We don't take the risk of having it installed by anyone else. I'll take you down to the factory while we're in Bath and you can meet them.' He frowned suddenly and picked up his pen, fiddling with it.

It was an unusual gesture for him. He was normally so very decisive and assured.

'What is it?' Claire asked.

'I was just thinking. If you're re-planning the bedrooms, it might be an idea for us to have interconnecting ones—I don't want any of our male guests getting the wrong idea.'

He meant that he didn't want his male pride hurt by others knowing that they didn't have a sexual relationship, Claire surmised, but she realised she was wrong when he said harshly, 'I don't want a repeat performance of what happened with Susie, Claire. I don't intend to lose you as well. If we have rooms at the opposite end of the house, you're bound to get some opportunist who's going to think that sexually you're as available as Susie was.

Neither of us wants that.'

She felt uncomfortably guilty when she realised that his concern had been as much for her as for himself. Every day, it seemed, she learned more about him, and the more she learned, the more she wondered how on earth Susie could have not loved him. Surely, if a woman could love a man it must be this one: he was caring and kind, attractive, considerate—and strong enough to lean on if one was the leaning type.

But he no longer wanted a woman's love, she reminded herself as she went to make them both a cup of coffee, so really it was just as well that she was incapable of giving him it.

In the scramble to get the girls and herself ready for an early start, mercifully Claire hadn't had much time to worry about the commitment she was about to make.

However, once she was inside the car, she had all the time in the world to worry about what she was doing.

Jay was a skilled but careful driver; the girls were both occupied with giggles and private chatter in the back; the music drifting from the stereo was designed to calm and relax; yet as the miles went by Claire found herself growing more and more tense, more and more convinced that she was doing the wrong thing, that she was, in fact, mad even to consider marrying. How on earth could it work?

'Stop worrying; everything will be fine, you'll see. Just think, in twenty-five years from today, you and I will be celebrating our silver wedding.'

His uncanny ability to divine her thoughts unnerved her. Unlike her, Jay seemed to have no doubts about the wisdom or the stability of their marriage , but then he already had something to compare it with, something to work towards, while she . . .

It was too late for second thoughts, Claire told herself firmly. She had already made a commitment to Heather, even though she hadn't yet made one to Jay, and on that count alone it was too late for going back.

Even so, she still found it hard to relax. Panic cramped through her stomach, an apprehension quite unlike any of her previous experiences enveloping her.

All the local weather seers had predicted a bad winter, and looking at the rolling countryside, held fast in the iron grip of a frost which turned the golden stubble monochrome, and lay across the bareness of the hedges like icing sugar, Claire could well believe that they were right.

In summer it was pretty countryside, but now the lavish display of autumn leaves had gone, and without the starkness that made harsher countryside look magnificent and awesome in winter, the bare fields only looked melancholic—or was that simply her imagination?

Just outside Bath, Jay turned off the main road, and drove in through an imposing gateway. Only a discreet plaque set into one of the brick pillars supporting the wrought iron gates betrayed that this was a hotel.

Beyond an avenue of bare trees Claire saw the house: soft cream Cotswold stone, the precision of a Georgian facacade.

A high wall joined what Claire suspected had originally been the stable block to the main

building, and Heather called out delightedly, 'Look
. . . it's just like *The Secret Garden*!'

'Look, Mummy, horses!' Lucy, wide-eyed,
tugged on her sleeve as she pressed her nose to the
car window. In a paddock opposite the house
several horses had gathered by the fence.

'There's a riding school here,' explained Jay.
'Lessons can be arranged for the guests.'

'Does that mean that we can ride?' breathed Lucy
expectantly.

Since their removal to the country, Lucy had
developed an intense passion for horses and ponies,
and Claire suppressed a faint sigh. 'Riding lessons
are very expensive, Lucy,' Claire cautioned, 'and
besides, Heather might not want to ride.'

'Yes, I do. I'd like a pony of my own. We both
would.'

'I think we're the victims of a two-pronged
attack,' Jay murmured *sotto voce* to Claire, but she
saw that he was smiling. 'We probably won't have
time for riding lessons while we're here,' he told
them, ignoring the protests of disappointment. 'But
maybe . . . maybe . . . if you're both very good,
Father Christmas . . .'

It was enough to produce ecstatic sighs of
anticipation, and to keep them quiet as Jay stopped
the car, and got out to go round and open Claire's
door.

'Don't worry about the luggage. Someone will
come out for it. Come on, you two,' he called to the
girls as they paused to give wistful glances in the
direction of the paddock.

'Heather's growing,' he murmured to Claire.

'Mmm. They both are,' but because, obviously,
no one had paid any attention to Heather's

wardrobe for quite a long time, her skirt was well above her small knees. 'It's going to prove an expensive couple of days,' Claire warned Jay. 'Both of them need new school clothes. Of course, I'll pay for Lucy's, but . . .'

'No.'

The sudden, unexpected pressure of his fingers on her arm shocked her into immobility. He was close enough for her to see the fine lines fanning out from his eyes—eyes that had gone cold and dark with anger. When he was like this he could be very forbidding indeed, she thought, noticing the way his mouth had hardened.

'No, Claire,' he said in a softer tone. 'I told you that from now on, financially, Lucy would be my responsibility, and I meant it. That's part of my contribution to our marriage; please don't deprive me of making it. I don't want to feel beholden to you any more than you do to me, you know. We're partners in this—equal partners.'

She knew that he was right.

He released her arm and she shivered suddenly, missing the protection of his tall body as he moved away from her, and a cold wind bit through her thin jacket.

'Come on, let's get inside; it's cold out here. Come on, you two,' he called to the girls. 'You can admire your new friends later.'

It was an odd sensation to have someone concerned for her comfort after being independent and alone for so long, even if he was only being courteous.

Inside, the hotel retained much of its country-house flavour. A smiling receptionist handed Jay a key, and called for a porter to show them the way to their suite. She was a pretty girl with blonde hair and nice teeth, and the way she smiled at Jay reminded Claire of just how sexually attractive he was. That knowledge seemed to heighten her own sense of inadequacy reminding her sharply of all that she wasn't and never could be.

But it was because of the things that she *was* that Jay was marrying her, she reminded herself firmly, and not the things she was not.

Their suite was magnificent: a sitting-room and three bedrooms, each with its own private bathroom, co-ordinated throughout in toning shades of French blue and terracotta. Here were several ideas she could copy for their own guest suites, and for the house itself, Claire reflected, making a closer examination of some decorative faux marbling on the door frames.

'What do you think of it?' Jay asked her, strolling over to join her as she studied the attractive décor of the sitting-room.

'It's lovely!'

'Yes. It certainly should be; they've spent a fortune on renovating the place.' He moved past her to look more closely at the delicate plasterwork on one of the walls, and instantly Claire realised.

'It's yours, isn't it? The plasterwork . . .'

He was grinning hugely, looking almost carefree.

'Yes, and the columns that have been marbled. I like the way they've done this, don't you?' he asked her, indicating a panel on the wall where the decorative plasterwork inside it had been delicately tinged in a soft terracotta fading to palest peach. 'I wonder how they do it.'

'By putting on the colour and then wiping it off.' Claire told him promptly. 'That way, only the most raised parts of the design get the paint.'

She saw his eyebrows lift and explained. 'It's something I'm very interested in, and last winter I got several books from the library on the subject. We could try something similar in the drawing-room, if you like, it's certainly large enough to take it.'

'Mummy, which bedroom is going to be ours?'

Lucy's impatient question distracted them both, and Claire suggested to her daughter that she and Heather should share the room with the two single beds in it.

While she was talking to them, the porter came up with their luggage. Jay tipped him and then glanced at his watch.

'It's gone twelve o'clock. How about an early lunch and then shopping this afternoon?' To Claire he added, 'We won't have time now, but later I'll show you the sports centre they have here. It's very luxurious, and we supplied the plaster columns that surround the swimming pool. We were called in after they had a bad fire eighteen months ago, and we had to replace and match a lot of the original plasterwork. This hotel is part of a small but very prestigious group which specialises in these country-house settings. We're in the process of negotiating a contract with them for work in other hotels owned by the group.'

He broke off suddenly and frowned, his voice brusque. 'I'm sorry, you don't want to hear all about that. It's boring . . .'

'It isn't boring at all,' Claire contradicted him quickly. 'I think it's fascinating.'

Jay gave her an odd look, and for the first time she saw in him Heather's vulnerability. She reached

out to touch his arm in the same comforting way she
would have done one of the girls, and as she touched
him, he stopped dead and stared down at her.
Immediately Claire withdrew from him, her face
scarlet.

'I'm sorry, I . . .'

'Don't be. There's no need.'

The way he was looking at her made her feel quite
odd, breathless and slightly light-headed, and then
the lift arrived and he looked away, and everything
returned to normal.

They lunched in what had once been the
Victorian conservatory, now beautifully restored
and replanted.

The menu, although not vegetarian, featured
recipes chosen with healthy eating in mind. Claire
and Jay both chose a vegetable mosaic in broccoli
mousse to start with, while the two girls opted for a
fresh fruit platter.

'What would you like for your main course?' Jay
asked her.

'I think I'll have the chicken in cheese sauce with
vegetables, and the same for the girls.'

'Mmm. I'm going to have the poached fillet of
steak.'

The food, when it came, was deliciously light,
leaving Claire feeling virtuous enough to opt for
crème caramel for her sweet.

Jay had ordered wine with their meal, and over
coffee Claire found herself slowly relaxing as the
alcohol spread through her body.

'It's just gone two now,' said Jay, glancing at his
watch. 'It will take us about twenty minutes to get
into Bath, so—if you're ready?'

At half past two exactly, he was skilfully parking

the car in the centre of Bath.

It was only a short walk from where they had
parked to the main shopping area, but Jay directed
them instead to what Claire soon realised was a far
more exclusive area.

'I'm told by my secretary that we're far more
likely to find what we want here,' was the only
explanation he gave Claire, as he shepherded them
all into one of the exclusive boutiques.

The woman who came forward to serve them was
wearing the most elegant casual clothes Claire had
ever seen, and her heart sank. It would cost a small
fortune to buy anything here. Jay probably didn't
realise. But Jay was already explaining to her that
she, Claire, needed a complete winter wardrobe,
including evening wear.

'There's a couple of toy shops further along here,'
he added to Claire. 'I'll take the girls there and they
can start thinking about what they'd like Father
Christmas to bring them. We'll come back in, say,
an hour.'

Whereas when he had calmly announced what he
thought she needed to buy she had felt almost
resentful, now, conversely, she felt as though he
were deserting her, and wanted to beg him to stay,
but he and the girls were gone before she could raise
any protest.

'What a sensible man your husband is,' remarked
the saleswoman when they had gone. 'Choosing
clothes is difficult enough, isn't it, without the
added distraction of an impatient family?'

'He isn't my husband,' Claire said weakly. 'At
least, not yet. We're getting married tomorrow.'

Now what on earth had made her say that? The
woman's semi-formal manner relaxed immediately.

'Oh, how exciting! Have you already chosen something to wear? Of course, I suppose you must...'

When Claire shook her head, she positively beamed.

'Well, you couldn't have chosen a better time to look, because we've just taken delivery of our winter stock. Let's get the basics out of the way first, shall we, and then we can concentrate on the "fancies". What does your own taste run to? Any particular make?'

Claire shook her head, unable to tell her that it was so long since she had bought herself anything that hadn't come from a chain store that she had no idea what to ask for.

'I like the outfit you're wearing,' she managed at last. 'But I'm afraid...'

'This is an Escada, and they do a lovely range. It's one of my favourites. I'll take you into our separates section and you can have a look. I'd say you were only a size 10, if that, so you won't be hard to fit.'

Half an hour later, Claire had chosen a slim-fitting grey skirt with a beautifully detailed silk satin blouse in cream, with padded shoulders that gave her a silhouette that she privately thought was almost film-star-ish. To go with it, the saleswoman suggested a sweater with a bird motif on it, in toning greys and creams, with a touch of blue to go with the very 'county' tweed jacket in the same range of colours.

Clare loved them all.

'It really is a "go anywhere" outfit,' the sales-woman told her, and Claire knew that she was right.

Having settled on them, the woman produced half a dozen day dresses in a variety of styles and

colours, and Claire allowed herself to be persuaded
into one in bright red, with a diamanté-speckled
bow at the throat and rows of demure pintucking
down to a dropped waist and slightly flared skirt. It
would be a lovely Christmas day dress, and luckily it
was the kind of red that she could wear. As this, too,
was added to the growing pile, she tried to stifle her
growing feeling of guilt. Surely Jay had never meant
her to spend so much money, but it seemed that he
had, because now the saleswoman was directing her
towards the evening clothes section of the shop,
which stretched a long way back from its small shop
window.

'I think this would suit you,' she told Claire,
producing a pretty blue knitted dress with a design
on it in sequins and bugle beads. 'This Frank Usher
is dressier—great for parties, and then we've a
range of cocktail suits.'

In the end Claire found she had added three more
outfits to the growing pile.

'Now, all that's left is your wedding outfit. Had
you anything in mind?'

When Claire shook her head, she smiled. 'Well, I
have! I'll show it to you.'

She came back with an outfit which she showed
to Claire. It was pure silk, with a pleated skirt and a
blouson top, and a ribbed waistline and cuffs. On
the white background was printed a design in soft
blue and terracotta, and Claire fell instantly in love
with it.

'Try it on,' the woman urged. 'It really is lovely.'

It was. The pleated skirt swayed and clung with
every step; the buttons up one side finished mid-
thigh so that every movement gave an enticing
glimpse of leg. The knitted cuff on the waistband of

the top ensured that it fitted snugly, and bloused properly, and Claire knew that if she searched for a month she could never find anything as attractive. But the price . . .

She was just about to refuse it when Jay and the girls walked in. She saw Jay in the mirror and noticed the way he came to an abrupt halt and just stared at her.

His stillness worried her, and she turned quickly to the saleswoman. 'It's lovely, but I'm afraid it's too expensive. I . . .'

'No. She's having it,' contradicted Jay flatly. 'I don't care how expensive it is,' he told Claire when she started to object. 'You're having it.'

'You looked very pretty in it, Mummy,' Lucy informed her when she re-emerged from the changing room. 'Didn't she, Heather?'

'Yes.'

'We've been in a toy shop, Mummy, and they had a doll's house, and teddies . . . and everything . . .'

'I seem to have spent an awful lot of money, Jay!' confessed Claire.

'I should hope so. That's why I brought you here. Dressing well will be part of your new role, Claire. If I couldn't afford it, you wouldn't be here. You'll need to get shoes, now, won't you and . . .'

'If I might recommend somewhere,' the saleswoman suggested, overhearing. 'There's a very good shop not very far away, and for good underwear, if I could suggest "Understudy"—it's only four doors away. They specialise in couture underwear.'

Claire could feel the heat crawling up under her skin. It was ridiculous to feel so embarrassed, but she did.

'Right, then,' said Jay when everything had been

packed and the bill paid. 'First underwear and then shoes.'

'Jay, you've spent so much already; I don't need . . .'

'What is it? Are you frightened that I might demand some sort of payment?'

She felt the blood leave her skin as Jay muttered the angry words in her ear.

'No . . . no, of course not. It's just . . .'

'Look, I've already tried to explain to you once, Claire: once you're my wife, you'll be expected to look the part. Susie always wore designer fashion; she . . .'

'I'm not Susie!'

Claire wasn't sure which of them was most surprised by her vehemence. Jay's mouth compressed slightly, his eyes flinty.

'No,' he agreed in a hard voice. 'You're not. And I wasn't making comparisons, if that's what you thought.'

Her small spurt of temper died as quickly as it had been born and Claire shook her head tiredly. 'No, I'm sorry. It's just that I feel so . . . overwhelmed . . .'

Try and think of it as buying a uniform for a new job,' he told her wryly. 'That might help.' They were outside the underwear shop already, and he pulled out his wallet and gave her a sum of money that made her eyes widen in shock.

'I think I can manage to keep the kids occupied for another half an hour. That should be long enough, shouldn't it?'

It was and when she re-emerged with several parcels, Claire marvelled at how quickly she had disposed of such a large sum of money.

'Shoes, and then somewhere to have a cup of tea before we start on the girls' things,' Jay pronounced as he took the packages from her. 'Don't worry, I'm not going to look,' he added drily, correctly interpreting her anxious look. It made her feel gauche and silly.

No doubt Susie had enjoyed not just buying but wearing wisps of lingerie for him. But their marriage wasn't going to be like that, she reminded herself, forcing down the panic that built up inside her every time she compared herself to his ex-wife. There was no need for her to worry. He didn't want another Susie . . . that was why he was marrying *her*.

CHAPTER SEVEN

'WAKE up, Mummy; it's time for breakfast.'

Claire opened protesting eyes and saw Lucy and Heather, both still in their dressing gowns, perched on her bed.

'Jay said we weren't to put on our new dresses until after breakfast.'

Wise Jay, Claire thought, struggling to sit up. Those delightful grey velvet dresses with their white collars and maroon velvet bows would not be enhanced by the addition of breakfast cereal. They had been shockingly expensive, but Jay had insisted on buying them, 'to wear for the wedding,' and then there had been those irresistible tartan dresses with white collars and matching bows that she hadn't been able to resist for Christmas Day; a red one for Heather with her dark colouring and a green one for Lucy who had inherited her chestnut hair.

'The man brought breakfast on a special table,' Lucy chattered on.

'But Daddy said we had to come and ask if you wanted a cup of tea,' added Heather.

'Ah, so you are awake!'

Jay stood in the doorway. He was wearing pyjama bottoms and a towelling robe—perfectly respectable articles of clothing, but nevertheless Claire felt her stomach clench and contract in response to the sight of him. He must have had a shower, because his hair was still damp.

126

'I believe it's tradition for the bride to have her breakfast in bed on her wedding day.'

'Not this bride,' Claire assured him firmly. 'I'm getting up. Come on, you two,' she told the girls, 'off the bed.' Her dressing gown lay just out of reach on a chair, and although her cotton nightshirt was perfectly respectable, she felt reluctant to get out of bed in front of Jay.

She was almost frozen with horror when he casually walked over to the chair and picked up her faded dressing-gown, holding it out to her.

As clearly as though she had spoken her anguish out loud, he came over to the bed, and said in a low voice so that the girls couldn't overhear,

'I'm not going to touch you, but there are going to be times when we're going to have to act the part of an apparently normally married couple. Children are very quick, and we don't want either of them worrying that something isn't right about our marriage. They'll accept the fact that we have separate rooms much more easily if they can see that we're on reasonably intimate terms. And the time to start establishing that is now, unless you want to be the object of village speculation and gossip.'

Claire knew that he was right. Even so, she wished he would move away from the bed, and more than that she wished that he would put down her robe and go away, but he wasn't going to. So she had to push back the covers and swing unsteady legs to the carpeted floor, trying to appear as casually relaxed as Jay was himself as he handed her her robe. As she turned to take it from him, his fingers rested on her arm, his mouth brushing a light kiss against her forehead. She could smell the clean mint freshness of his breath, and the soapiness of his body.

The reality of him was so different from her deeply suppressed memories of her attacker that it held her tense with surprise.

She heard him say her name, but wasn't aware of the harsh undertone to his voice until his grip on her arm tightened and she focused on him.

His eyes were brilliant with an anger that made her recoil sharply. 'No ... Claire ...' His grip prevented her from breaking free. 'I'm sorry. The look on your face brought home to me what could have happened to Heather. I think it takes being a father to bring home to a man how vulnerable and unprotected women are. I think if any man hurt either Heather or Lucy I would tear him apart with my bare hands. I wish I could turn time back for you and wipe out what happened, but I can't ...'

'No ... And at least I have Lucy,' Claire said unsteadily.

The emotion in his eyes and voice had been so unexpected. His fingers still dug into her arm and she covered them gently.

'I'm sorry, did I hurt you? I ...' He sounded almost dazed.

'It doesn't matter.'

Heather and Lucy had disappeared into the sitting-room, but now Heather came back, hovering uncertainly in the doorway, eyeing them both with an anxiety that tore at Claire's heart.

'Susie never liked her interrupting us,' muttered Jay huskily when he saw Claire's frown. 'In some way she almost seemed to be jealous of any attention I gave her.'

Understanding the reason for the little girl's

hesitation, Claire smiled at her. 'Come on, let's all have breakfast,' she suggested cheerfully. 'After all, we've got a wedding to go to.'

Contrary to all her expectations, the civil ceremony, far from being austere and unmeaningful, took place in a small, prettily decorated room. Cn the registrar's desk was a bowl of fresh flowers, and Claire had the feeling that everything that could be done had been done to make the room attractive and welcoming. The service, simple though it was, was very moving, causing even Lucy to remain silent in awareness of the solemnity of the occasion.

Jay didn't kiss her, and she was glad of that. Her nerves were too tightly strung to endure much more.

A cold wind knifed through her thin suit as they all walked outside. Claire saw Jay frown and put out an arm as though he intended to draw her close to his side to keep her warm, and she moved away from him automatically, shivering as she felt the wind bite.

'You need a coat.'

'I've already got one,' she told him lightly. It was true, she had; an ancient duffle-coat which she had bought second-hand but which was excellent at keeping out the cold.

'Now that you're married, will Jay be my daddy?' Lucy demanded irrepressibly as Jay led the way back to the car.

Over her head Jay looked at Claire. Stooping down to the little girl's height, he asked her quietly, 'Would you like me to be your daddy, Lucy?'

Her emphatic 'Yes,' would have made Claire smile at any other time.

'And Heather wants you to be her mummy,' she told Claire firmly.

Claire bit her lip and looked helplessly at Jay. Heather already had a mother.

'I think it will be easier all round if we let both girls call us "Mummy" and "Daddy",' he suggested softly.

'But Heather . . .'

'I want you to be my mummy,' Heather protested, clinging to Claire's arm and gazing up at her, and Claire didn't have the heart to deny her.

Whatever happened though, she promised herself, if Heather ever wanted to talk about her mother, and to see her, she would do her utmost to ensure that she did. Maybe now, with Susie's rejection of her very much to the forefront of her mind, she didn't want to know about her natural mother, but later, when she was more adult . . . It was something she would have to discuss with Jay, Claire admitted to herself, but not right now.

'Who's hungry?' asked Jay, lightening the emotional mood. 'I've booked us into a local restaurant for lunch,' he told Claire. 'I felt we should do something to celebrate, but I also thought you might not like the idea of the hotel staff knowing that we'd just got married.'

His sensitivity, so unexpected in so tough a man, made her eyes sting with emotional tears. It seemed unbelievable that a man who had so many demands on his time already should make the effort to arrange a celebratory luncheon for what, after all, to him was merely a business arrangement.

The restaurant was in a small village several miles outside Bath. The chef had trained with the

Roux brothers, Jay informed Claire as they drew up outside.

The restaurant had once been a farmhouse, and a huge log fire burned in the enormous hearth, throwing out a welcome heat. The furniture was simple and cottagey, the beamed walls colour-washed a soft cream, the old rose carpet on the floor enhancing the intimate atmosphere of the place.

They were shown to a table slightly secluded from the others, a deferential waiter ceremoniously unfolding the crisply starched pink napkins and placing them on two grey velvet laps, much to the awed delight of the girls.

'I've already ordered our meal,' Jay explained. 'So if there's anything you don't like . . .' He broke off as another waiter advanced with an ice bucket and two glasses.

'Champagne,' he told Claire quietly. 'I felt it was appropriate.'

Champagne! It was the last thing she had expected, and she sipped the golden wine nervously, gasping as the ice-cool liquid bubbled down her throat.

'Like it?'

'It's lovely! I've never had any before.' She flushed, wondering what on earth Jay must think of a woman of her age who had never tasted champagne, but he looked more sombre than amused.

'You can drink it with your first course,' he told her, 'I'll order wine to have with the main meal.'

'Mummy, what's that you're drinking?' Lucy demanded, and when Claire told her, she said eagerly, 'May I have some?'

She was just about to refuse, when Jay summoned

a waiter and said something to him. Within seconds
he returned and put down two glasses of fresh
orange juice, to which he added a very small
amount of champagne before handing them to the
girls.

Watching Lucy's beatific expression as she
sipped her drink, Claire could only marvel at how
much Jay had enriched their lives already.

'You're spoiling them. You're spoiling all of us,'
she remonstrated.

'A little bit of spoiling once in a while never did
anyone any harm.'

It was mid-afternoon before they left the restaurant. Claire had eaten caviare, and truffles, and
vegetables so perfectly fresh that the flavour had
been indescribable. It was a meal she would never
forget, even if it had not marked their wedding
ceremony, and she shuddered to think how much it
had all cost.

'Feel like a quick trip round the factory before we
go back to the hotel, or would you prefer to go
straight back?'

'I'd like to see round the factory,' Claire told him
eagerly. The more she saw of Jay's work, the more
eager she was to see how it was produced.

Jay's factory was situated in a purpose-built
modern building on the edge of an industrial estate.
His small work-force treated Claire deferentially
but with reserve until they realised that she was
genuinely interested in their work, and then it was
as though the floodgates had opened.

These were craftsmen, Claire realised, listening
to them—men who took a pride in what they were
doing, and who believed that what they were
creating today would be the heirlooms of tomorrow.

'You haven't forgotten that you're taking us to the zoo tomorrow, Mummy, have you?' demanded Lucy sleepily later on that evening after she and Heather had been put to bed.

They had all dined together in the suite, and then they had watched television together.

At first Claire had felt uncomfortably aware of her changed status, but Jay's manner towards her was so calm and matter-of-fact that her tension had gradually gone. Now she felt pleasantly tired.

'I don't know about you, but I feel that an early night is in order,' he remarked easily when she went back into the sitting-room.

'I agree, especially bearing in mind tomorrow's trip to the zoo!'

Jay had stood up as she walked into the room, but he made no move towards her as she walked across to her own bedroom.

'I'll say goodnight, then,' she said gravely, pausing outside it.

'Yes. Sleep well.'

So now she was married, Claire thought flatly as she closed her bedroom door behind her. What was Jay thinking right now? Was he comparing tonight to his first wedding night—comparing her to Susie?

Stop it, she chided herself. Jay married you because he doesn't want another relationship like the one he had with Susie.

They had a fortnight of relatively uninterrupted peace, with Jay commuting daily to the factory, and then he came home one night and announced that he had to go back to the States.

'Apparently there are a couple of points in the contract they want to discuss. I shouldn't be gone

for too long. I might even pick up some additional
business! Apparently my client's sister wants to talk
to me about remodelling her indoor swimming pool
and its surroundings, using our stuff. If all goes well
I ought to be back by the end of the week.'

They all went with him to the airport to see him
off, and then Claire got a taxi back to Bath. With
nearly a whole day to spare, she was determined to
make a start on her plans for the house.

The blue and terracotta colour scheme at the
hotel had fired her imagination, and already she
had a few tentative ideas of what she wanted to do,
but first she needed to find someone to help her, and
she remembered seeing a small shop in Bath which
had advertised an interior design service.

She found it easily enough and paused outside to
admire the window. A bolt of material was draped
carelessly over a single chair; an arrangement of
toning dried flowers displayed next to it on a pastel-
toned kilim rug.

Feeling slightly apprehensive, Claire went inside,
warning Lucy and Heather not to touch anything.

A smiling blonde woman came to serve her.
Slightly plump, and in her mid-thirties, she looked
as elegant as her window.

It didn't take Claire long to outline her ideas, and
within minutes of being shown wallpaper pattern
books and swatches of fabrics, she knew that she
had found someone on her own wavelength.

'What I'd really like is for you to come out to the
house,' she confided. 'I don't want to employ an
interior designer as such, because I want the house
to reflect our own taste. I want it to be a home, not a
show place, but I need advice on where I can find

the right kind of decorators—you know the sort of thing.'

'Yes, I do, and most of my clients feel the same way that you do. There is a move away from the very traditional interior design service now, to one where we work alongside the client.' She picked up a diary. 'I could come out on Thursday morning if that's any good.'

'That's fine.' Claire gave her directions, and left the shop feeling buoyed up with achievement.

It had occurred to her that since Jay's craftsmen could make panelling and bookcases, they must also be able to craft kitchen units for her, and on impulse, instead of going straight home, she asked her taxi driver to call at the factory on the way.

The foreman remembered her and made her welcome. When Claire explained what she wanted, he readily agreed that it was something they could do.

'Any work in hand would have to take precedence, of course,' Claire acknowledged, 'but what I had in mind was something in antique pine?'

'You're in luck there. Jay recently bought up some old pine doors from a demolition site. I'll have to check with him that he doesn't have something in mind for them, of course.'

Hastily concurring with this, Claire left it that once Jay had returned, and if he was in agreement, someone could come out to the house to measure up for her kitchen.

She had already decided that in the girls' room she would have fitted walls and cupboards built which could then be painted and decorated with stencils, and that in the guest rooms, the same simple type of built-in furniture could be marbled,

dragged, or sponged in a variety of paint finishes to
create a very luxurious effect.

The displays in some of the shop windows
reminded her that Christmas wasn't very far away.
She already had a fair idea of what both girls
wanted, and she and Jay had already talked over the
idea of riding lessons and then possibly a pony to
share if their enthusiasm lasted.

This would be the first Christmas that she had
not had to scrimp to buy Lucy even the simplest
present. She glanced down at her daughter's
burnished head. Already she could see the differ-
ence in Lucy; she was a little girl who needed a
masculine influence in her life, and she adored Jay.
Heather, too, had blossomed, and now she chattered as happily as Lucy, as both of them drew her
attention to a shop window filled with a cornucopia
of childish delights.

The bright sunny day had given way to a frosty
evening when they eventually got back to the house.
After supper, when Claire was tidying up, the
phone rang.

When she picked it up and heard Jay's voice, she
was almost too stunned to speak. They chatted for
several minutes, mostly about the children, and
even though she had not been expecting the call,
when he eventually rang off she felt curiously
bereft.

What would he be doing tonight? Would he be
alone in his hotel room, or, far more likely, would he
be out somewhere being wined and dined? And
then afterwards, would he . . .?

Angry with herself, she pushed the thought away.
She had no right to question the very personal side
of Jay's life. If he chose to go to bed with someone

that was no concern of hers. So why was there this unpleasant little ache inside her? Shaking her head, she switched off the lights and made her way slowly upstairs. The house felt empty without him. Already she missed him; she missed his company at supper, missed hearing about his days, missed their chats by the fire after dinner.

He came back at the end of the week, and the whole house seemed to come alive. Both little girls flung themselves at him the moment he opened the door, and Claire saw in the look he gave her over their heads that he was pleased with the change in Heather.

After dinner he told her about his trip. She learned that in addition to the contract which was now due to be signed after the New Year, he had also received commissions from several of his client's friends and from his sister.

When Claire enthused he frowned.

'Yes, it's good for business, but it does mean I'm going to be away quite a lot, although I hope only for the next few weeks.'

'Well, the girls will be pleased,' she remarked drily, 'especially if you keep spoiling them with presents like those you brought back this time.'

The huge patchwork dolls Jay had brought back with him from Dallas were so exquisitely detailed that Claire felt they were more for just looking at than playing with, and she knew, just from the workmanship, that they must have been horrendously expensive.

'Guilty conscience presents,' he explained, frowning suddenly as he added, 'which reminds me.' He got up. 'I won't be a minute. Wait here.'

He was back almost immediately carrying a large

manilla envelope which he gave to her.

'Your wedding present,' he told her quietly.

Claire opened it and took out the contents, smoothing them with suddenly tense fingers. She read through the papers once again and then again just to make sure she wasn't making any mistakes.

'You're paying for the work to be done on the cottage! But it will cost thousands! Jay, you mustn't feel you need to do that . . .'

'I wanted to do it. Let's face it, Claire, I could have offered to pay for the damage in the first place, then you wouldn't have needed to marry me.' He held up his hand when she would have interrupted. 'No, I'm not implying that you married me purely for material reasons—I know how much you love Heather—but you have to admit that it was an excellent lever, and I used it deliberately. In fact, that storm couldn't have come at a better time as far as I was concerned. If you hadn't had to move in here, we would have had to have a long courtship, with all its attendant problems, and for selfish reasons I wanted our marriage accomplished fast. I've already made the mistake of trapping one woman into marriage; I wanted to give you an escape route if you ever felt you needed it. I was going to suggest that when the work is complete you let the cottage—everyone likes to have their own financial independence; it won't bring in much, but at least it will be yours.'

His sensitivity made her want to weep. How long had it been since a man, any man, had shown her such consideration, such care?

Almost without thinking she leaned forward, touching the side of his face with her fingers. 'Oh, Jay, I just don't know what to say!'

He turned his head, his fingers clasping her wrist, and she gasped as she felt the warm pressure of his mouth against the palm of her hand.

The moment she tensed he released her.

'Sorry.' His voice sounded gruff. 'I'd forgotten.'

'It . . . it doesn't matter. I'll go and make some coffee.' Claire stood up shakily and hurried into the kitchen. How on earth could she have explained to him that her tension had come not from the warm contact of his mouth against her palm, but from her own totally unexpected reaction to it? She had liked it; she had enjoyed the totally pleasurable sensation that had shot through her body.

He was at home for five days, just enough time to go shopping with the girls to buy advent calendars, and to keep them occupied while Claire sneaked their carefully chosen presents into the house. And then he was gone. Back to Dallas to discuss the final details of the contract.

The American client was a builder, specialising in prestigious new houses, for which he wanted only the finest craftsmanship. Of a neo-Georgian design, their proportions lent themselves well to the reproduction plasterwork Jay's company produced, but the American lawyers were finicking over every detail, and so Jay and his solicitor had to fly out once again.

It worried Claire how much she missed him. She oughtn't to have done; after all, she had never wanted a husband—but Jay wasn't just a husband, he was a person who made her laugh, who treated her as an equal, who filled out and warmed her life in a way she could never have believed possible.

She went with him to the airport, where he was meeting his solicitor, and was surprised by the sudden surge of desolation that struck her as he walked away. She wanted to cling on to him, to . . . Abruptly her body tensed as she watched his retreating back. Confusion and panic replaced desolation. What was happening to her? She mustn't become emotionally dependent on Jay as well as financially dependent on him.

The days flew by, excitement mounting as the girls opened door after door on their advent calendars. They were both in the school play—nearly everyone in the school was involved in it in one way or another. Claire went to see them, and took Mrs Vickers with her because Jay was still away.

The last few days before Christmas trickled away far too fast. Jay rang three days before Christmas Eve to warn her that he could only get home at the last minute. Claire, who had put off buying and dressing a tree in the hope that he would be home in time, took the girls to the local garden centre and they chose one together, but it wasn't the same as it would have been if Jay had been with her.

After Christmas, work would start on the house, but until then she had warmed up the sitting-room with deep pink and blue satinised-cotton-covered cushions and a large, toning rug.

But without Jay in it the house lacked something Claire recognised; she missed his vibrantly masculine presence. A trickle of awareness ran down her spine, a sense of danger and unease. She didn't want to miss Jay, to be so conscious of his absences. She dismissed her thoughts as foolish, but something lingered, some faint frisson of knowledge that she determinedly forced into the back of her mind to think about later—much, much later.

CHAPTER EIGHT

THE night before Christmas Eve, they decorated the tree. Claire sat looking at it after the girls had gone to bed, watching the soft dazzle of the tiny pinpoints of light. Everything was ready: the presents were wrapped, including the appallingly expensive desk filing system she had bought for Jay, the turkey was keeping cold in the garage, all the shopping was done, and for once even the weather was in tune with the season. It had been cold all day, and now the night sky had a dull glow that presaged snow.

Everything was ready, but Jay was not here to share it with them. She told herself that she was disappointed for the girls, that it was because of them that that small ball of pain lodged deep inside her wouldn't go away.

She stretched tiredly and got up to tidy away the debris from the tree decorations. Perhaps if she made some mince pies that might help relax her.

She went into the kitchen and was soon busily engaged in the ritual of making pastry. Through the window she saw the first flakes of snow fall, and was unable to resist the childish impulse to watch. Thick, fat snowflakes fell from a midnight blue sky, whirling and dancing in a pattern that mesmerised her. A fine white blanket covered the ground before she managed to drag herself away.

Snow for Christmas. She finished making her

mince pies and put them in the oven.

It was still snowing half an hour later when the pies were cooling on a rack and she had finished cleaning the kitchen. It was too early to go to bed, but she felt too keyed up to sit down and watch television or read a book.

She was just about to make herself a cup of hot chocolate when the back door suddenly opened.

'Jay!' She said his name unsteadily, unable to believe it was him. The snow must have muted the sound of his car. Snowflakes clung to his hair and jacket.

Somehow, without knowing how it had happened, she had crossed the kitchen floor, her face alight with pleasure.

She touched his arm and grimaced. 'You're all cold and wet!' She was standing so close to him that when she looked up she could see the dark irises of his eyes. As she looked his expression changed and she felt a strange tension grip her.

'You're . . . you're back early . . .'

Her voice sounded rusty, and she seemed to be having difficulty breathing.

'I managed to get an earlier flight; Christmas is no time to be away from home. Girls in bed?'

'Yes. Over an hour ago.'

For some reason she felt oddly flat. She moved away from him, checking as he laid his hand on her arm.

'Claire.'

She turned towards him, her eyes widening as he bent his head and she felt the warm brush of his mouth against her own. It was an odd sensation, that soft touch of warm lips. It made her quiver inside, and realise on a searing wave of pain that never once in her life had she been kissed properly.

The sudden shocking hiss of boiling milk spilling on to the cooker jolted her back to reality, her body stiffening with rejection and fear. Immediately Jay released her.

'I'm sorry.' He sounded weary. 'For a moment I forgot . . . .'

What had he forgotten? That he wasn't coming home to Susie? 'It doesn't matter . . .'

She just caught the expression of grimness tightening his mouth before he turned away.

'I was just making myself a cup of chocolate. Would you like one . . . or something to eat?' she asked hurriedly.

'These smell good.'

He had obviously recognised her conciliatory offer and was trying to respond to it, Claire realised as he picked up one of her mince pies and ate it.

'Chocolate will be fine, and then an early night, I think. I ate on the plane.'

'Shall we drink it in the sitting-room?'

Those few moments of strained intimacy might never have occurred. On the surface all was as it had always been, but beneath that surface Claire was just beginning to realise that there lurked some very treacherous waters indeed.

What would have happened if the milk hadn't boiled over? Would he have gone on kissing her? Would she have let him . . .? It was too uncomfortable an avenue of thought for her to pursue.

'You go through; I'll bring the chocolate in a minute.'

The faintly sardonic look he gave her made her face burn. Did he realise how odd his proximity was making her feel? She felt that she needed to be alone

to get herself back to normal. That brief pressure of
his mouth against hers had unleashed a series of
sensations she was still having difficulty coming to
terms with.

It hadn't been dislike or fear she had felt in those
few seconds before reality had intruded, far from it.
So, what had she felt? Shock, grief for all that was
missing from her life, and also a frisson of pleasure
so delicate and new to her that even now she wasn't
sure if she had experienced it or merely imagined it.
But surely it was impossible to imagine something
like that—something she had never known before
in her life, or dreamed of knowing? Now she had
known it.

Shaking herself free of her confusing thoughts,
she put the two mugs of chocolate on a tray and
added a plate of mince pies, quickly making some
sandwiches from the ham she had roasted that
morning.

Jay was sitting on the settee when she walked in,
his head relaxed against the cushions. 'I like the
tree,' he commented, getting up to pull up one of the
small coffee-tables for her to put the tray on.

The room had an open fireplace with an immense
cream marble surround, part of the original
Victorian architecture. Susie had had the fireplace
blocked off, and one of the first things Claire had
done was to have it re-opened and an attractive coal
effect gas fire installed. She switched it on, and
paused for a moment to watch the flickering flames.

'Mmm . . . very cosy.' An expression of sadness
seemed to cloud Jay's eyes.

'The girls wanted to wait until you came home to
decorate it, but I thought you might be too late.'

'There's nothing on the top.'

'I couldn't reach,' Claire confessed. 'There's a fairy in the box that the girls chose.'

'I'll put it on for them tomorrow. Mmm, these are good.'

He was eating one of the sandwiches she had made. Without his suit jacket and his shirt open at the throat he looked less formidable. He was tired, she realised.

'How did it go in Dallas?' she asked.

'Come and sit down here beside me and I'll tell you.'

She sat next to him on the sofa.

'What an excellent wife you are, Claire: caring, obedient . . .'

At first she thought he was mocking her and she flushed painfully and started to move away, his hand on her arm stopping her.

'What's the matter?'

'I know . . . I'm not Susie,' she said painfully. 'It can't be much . . . fun for you coming home to me, Jay . . .'

'Fun?' His mouth twisted bitterly. 'Is that what you think Susie and I had, Claire? There's nothing fun about coming home to find your wife's out enjoying herself with another man, while your child is left all alone. There's nothing fun about knowing she's being unfaithful, about knowing she doesn't give a damn. I never caught an early flight to come home to Susie, Claire, because I never knew what I was coming home to. If you want the truth, I dreaded coming home.'

His mouth compressed, his eyes focusing on the leaping flames of the fire, as he looked back into the past.

'Don't ever think I'm comparing you with

Susie—there is no comparison.'

No, there wasn't, Claire realised. He had loved and desired Susie, while she was just someone whom he had chosen to marry because of Heather.

'I have to go back to Dallas after the New Year, and I want you and the girls to come too. John and his wife want to meet you.'

'Me—but . . .?'

'It's the American way,' he told her laconically. 'They're throwing a big party to celebrate the signing of the contract and we're invited to be their house guests. It will be during the school holidays, so it shouldn't be too much of a problem.'

Jay moved to pick up his mug of chocolate, the muscles down his back and arm tautening. His skin where it was exposed by the collar and cuff of his shirt was brown and firm, his wrist very sinewy in comparison to hers.

'This will be Heather's first real Christmas; Susie always preferred to go away somewhere.' He put down his empty mug and relaxed back against the cushions. Somehow he seemed to have moved closer to her, but she felt no compulsion to move away.

'You look tired.'

He turned his head and she saw the small darker flecks in his eyes. 'I am,' he admitted. He closed his eyes and sighed. 'It was quite a shock to come home and find snow.'

'My first white Christmas.'

He made a sound in his throat that might have meant anything and Claire turned to look at him. His eyes were closed and she sensed that he was on the verge of falling asleep.

She got up to take their cups to the kitchen, and

when she came back he was fast asleep, sprawled
out against the sofa. She leaned over him shaking
him gently.

'Jay . . .'

'Mmm.'

The shock of his arms coming round her and
pulling her down against the relaxed warmth of his
body was totally unexpected. Her knees had caught
against the edge of the sofa so that she had collapsed
on to him, and now he was burrowing his face into
the curve of her neck, his breath triggering off tiny
convulsive waves of sensation where it touched her
skin.

After her initial moment of panic, what she felt
was nothing like the terror and disgust she had
experienced before. Being held in Jay's arms was so
totally different from that. She felt at once both safe
and yet deliciously trembly, her body fitting softly
against the hard planes of his.

He was cuddling up to her in much the same way
that Heather held on to her teddy, she thought with
shaky amusement, and she had no doubt that he
was totally oblivious to what he was doing. It would
have been the easiest thing in the world to wake him
up and break out of his hold of her, but for some
reason she felt no compulsion to do so. Instead she
raised her hand tentatively and touched the stubbly
line of his jaw, held deep in thrall to a curious need
to know more of the alien maleness of him. He
muttered something in his sleep, releasing her
momentarily as he raised his hand to cover hers, his
head turning so that he could caress the soft skin of
her palm with his mouth. The sensation that shot
through her was so totally unexpected, so thoroughly unnerving, that she jerked back instinctively.

Instantly Jay was awake, his eyelids lifting, although he didn't move. His cheekbone pressed hard against her shoulder, and she was acutely conscious of him in a thousand previously unknown ways. As though some deep inner part of her was waking from a long sleep, she felt the first stirrings of what she sensed instinctively was her suppressed sexuality.

Fear, joy, an exhilaration beyond anything she had previously known quivered through her; she felt as though she wanted to get up and dance, to burst out into a song of pleasure, to open her heart to him and tell him about the miracle his touch had somehow achieved. Because to her it was a miracle that for the first time since she was attacked she had felt like a woman.

A great flood of joy filled her. She wanted to reach out and touch him to communicate to him in all the ways there were her sense of release and freedom, but already he was withdrawing from her, his expression shuttered, as he said curtly,

'Sorry about that, Claire. I didn't mean to touch you.'

It was like someone cruelly puncturing a gaily coloured balloon. One moment it was a thing of joy and beauty floating free; the next it was gone. She came down to earth with his curt words ringing in her head, and she shivered violently, suddenly realising her own folly.

Jay had married her because she wasn't a sexual woman, and she must not let herself forget that. He didn't want the complications of any sort of emotional relationship with her, and for her a relationship in the physical sense would have to contain an element of emotional commitment as well.

A physical relationship? What on earth was she thinking? Her face went white with the shock of the realisation that hit her. She licked her lips nervously, unaware of her state of frozen tension or of the interpretation Jay was putting on her stiff silence.

'Look, Claire, it won't happen again. It was a momentary aberration, nothing more.' He got up and paced the floor tensely. 'Try and put it out of your mind.'

What was he saying to her? Her confused mind tried to sort out the meaning of the words, and failed.

'I . . . I think I ought to go to bed.'

She got up, still trembling wildly, retreating from him when he reached out to help her.

Jay watched her as she fled from the room, and then walked over to the fireplace, to stare moodily out of the darkened window. In front of it the tree glimmered softly in all its finery, but he didn't see it.

A frustrated bitterness glittered in his eyes as he turned to face his own reflection in the giltwood mirror above the fireplace.

'Damn!' he swore savagely, bringing his fist down on to the marble with a force that threatened to crack the bones. 'Damn . . . and damn again . . .'

On Christmas morning they were up early, despite the fact that Claire and Jay had attended Midnight Mass the night before.

Both girls had had small stockings filled with little presents left at the bottom of their beds the night before, but Claire had already stipulated that the rest of the presents, which were piled beneath

the tree, were not to be opened until after breakfast.
She suspected that was the only way of making sure
that Heather and Lucy got something inside them.

There had been another fall of snow, and there
had been a magical quality to their walk through the
village to the pretty Norman church the night
before. Jay, in a fit of impulsive extravagance, had
insisted on buying a huge red wooden sledge for the
girls on Christmas Eve, and that too was now
wrapped up beneath the tree alongside the dolls'
pram Heather had asked for, and Lucy's bike.

Claire had spent almost every evening in Decem-
ber knitting small woolly garments for the golden-
haired doll who was to occupy the pram, and
against her better judgment both girls were to
receive the much desired, and to Claire's mind,
quite revolting pastel-haired plastic ponies they had
both ecstatically requested.

Tastes change, she reminded herself, as she heard
the squeals of pleasure coming from their room, and
no doubt she had pleaded for things that her parents
had found equally incomprehensible.

She was still smiling about this when her
bedroom door opened, but it wasn't the girls who
came in, it was Jay, a towelling robe belted over his
pyjama bottoms, a cup of tea and some digestive
biscuits on the tray he was carrying.

The awkwardness she had anticipated having to
cope with after the evening of his return had never
materialised. In the morning Jay had been as
casually relaxed as he had always been, and she had
been too busy to give more than a passing thought to
her own reaction to him. In fact she had begun to
think she had imagined it, but the way her heart
jerked like a stranded fish just because he walked

into her room told her better.

'You're looking very flushed,' he commented, completely misreading her vivid blush. 'Not sickening for a cold, are you? Those boots you were wearing last night . . .'

The boots in question were old ones, but they were good enough for the snow.

'I'm fine,' she told him, watching him put the tray down on her bedside table, before he perched himself on the edge of the bed.

'Mmm. You were looking very perky when I came in. You were grinning like a Cheshire Cat!'

'I was thinking about those awful ponies we bought for the girls and wondering if I ever wanted something that appalled my parents.'

'Well, I know I did,' confessed Jay. 'My parents were both members of CND, and one year I asked Father Christmas for a tank and sub-machine gun. It says a lot for their understanding that I got both— I also got twelve months' worth of lectures from my mother, pointing out the savagery of war.'

He didn't often talk about his family, possibly because the subject had never come up, and Claire had not liked to question him.

'What happened to them?' she asked now.

'My mother was killed in a rail accident in France and my father died of a heart attack not long afterwards. I was the only one, and away at university at the time. I missed them, of course, but I think it's only when one becomes a parent oneself that one realises the true depth of parental love.'

'Yes. They say, don't they, that it's the mark of a successful parent to be able to send out one's young to enjoy the world without them having to give you a backward glance. The security of a loving background——'

'Helps to create a child who is healthily selfish in its attitude to its parents. Yes, I know. You've done wonders with Heather,' Jay added quietly. 'She's a different child.'

'She just needed more self-confidence. Heather knows I love her, and because of that . . .'

'She can love herself . . .' He broke off and grimaced as two small bodies came hurtling into the room.

'Downstairs, the pair of you,' he told them. 'We're going to make breakfast for Mummy this morning.'

They were wearing their new tartan dresses, and Claire felt her throat lock with emotional tears as she saw the matching tartan bows tied in their hair. Both of them wanted to grow their hair, and for school she made them wear it plaited. This morning both of them sported rather drunken bows.

'Heather put my ribbon in my hair for me,' announced Lucy cheerfully, darting past Jay to climb on to the bed.

'And Lucy did mine.' Heather, not to be outdone, climbed on the other side, still clutching her stocking.

'Look what Father Christmas brought me . . .'

'And me . . .'

'Something tells me if I want any breakfast, I'm going to have to make it on my own,' smiled Jay.

'I'll be down in a minute,' Claire assured him, shooing both girls off the bed.

'Mummy, have you got a new dress to wear too?'

She was going to wear the pretty red one she had bought in Bath. The girls' excitement was infectious, and Claire felt it bubble up inside her as she showered and dressed.

When she got down to the kitchen, Heather and Lucy were happily tucking into bowls of creamy porridge. Jay had made the coffee, and the rich smell of it floated aromatically on the air.

'Can I leave you in charge while I go up and get dressed?'

'Don't be long, will you, Daddy?' Heather demanded impatiently.

It was impossible to keep the girls at the table after they had finished eating. They had already seen the pile of brightly wrapped presents surrounding the tree, and Jay and Claire exchanged amused looks over their heads as they hurried Jay to finish his toast.

'You're looking very festive,' he murmured to her as they followed the girls to the sitting-room. 'Red suits you.'

He was wearing a pair of mid-blue trousers that clung to the hard muscles of his thighs. His checked woollen shirt was open at the throat, the softness of the cashmere sweater he was wearing over it touching Claire's skin as the girls dashed past them and she was forced to move closer to his side.

If having one child at Christmas time was fun, having two was more than double the pleasure. As she remembered her pathetic attempts to make something special out of Christmas for Lucy when she was a baby, Claire thought wistfully of the delight it would be to be able to watch that wide-eyed joy and bewilderment now, in these warm protected surroundings.

Lucy's first Christmas had been in the cold damp of their flat, her first Christmas tree one Claire had salvaged at a jumble sale. Expensive presents didn't make Christmas, she knew that, but warmth, comfort, security; these all added an indefinable lustre of pleasure to this special time of year.

For a few seconds there was pandemonium as sheet after sheet of wrapping paper was shredded in their wild attempts to discover what was inside, but Claire had deliberately given them the much desired ponies first, and once they had assured themselves that Father Christmas had not been remiss in this regard, they settled down quite contentedly to savour the rest of their booty.

Claire, who had not been expecting any presents at all, was surprised to discover that she had quite a pile, two of them very inexpertly wrapped, and decorated with stick-on home-made Christmas trees.

'We made those for you,' Heather told her importantly. 'Daddy helped us.'

It brought a lump to her throat to think of Jay finding precious time to assist with the choosing and wrapping of her presents. Another man could quite easily have carelessly ignored the sensitive feelings of two very feminine six-year-olds and had them gift-wrapped instead. Even though she prided herself on being practical, Claire knew quite well that those lovingly made wrappings would find their way into the large cardboard box in which she hoarded all her sentimental treasures.

This was the first year Lucy had had someone to assist her with such a task, and as she looked into her daughter's shining eyes as she unwrapped the soap and bath oil she had chosen, she felt a tremendous surge of gratitude and joy.

This marriage was right; right for Heather and

Lucy and right for her. But was it right for Jay? a tiny inner voice asked her. Would he come to regret his selflessness in putting Heather's needs before his own?

'Smell it, Mummy,' urged Lucy. 'I chose it specially, because it reminded me of you.'

Rather cautiously Claire took the top off the bath oil, and was surprised to discover that despite its rather virulent colour it smelled pleasantly of roses.

'Now mine,' Heather instructed, watching her with anxious eyes as she carefully unwrapped her second untidy parcel.

'We saved up with our spending money,' Lucy explained importantly. 'Daddy saved it for us, didn't you?'

Although Heather had been calling her 'Mummy' for some time, and had indeed anxiously asked to be allowed to do so, this was the first time Lucy had referred to Jay as 'Daddy'.

Wondering if Jay was as aware of this completely natural acceptance of him as she was herself, Claire glanced across at him, and saw that he shared her feelings.

In a moment of shared intimacy and awareness they continued to look at one another, and Claire experienced a closeness to him that made her feel both exalted and humble.

'Look at mine,' Heather urged her impatiently, tugging on her sleeve. 'Look at mine!'

The moment was gone, but Claire knew that she would remember and savour it later.

Heather had bought her body lotion and talc to go with Lucy's soap and bath oil. Overcome with emotion, Claire held out her arms to both of them,

hugging them tightly. Lucy, as always, was the first
to break free.

'Daddy hasn't opened his present yet,' she said
severely.

'Something tells me that Father Christmas has
been extremely active on my behalf this year,'
drawled Jay, looking at Claire. It was true that she
had found several small things to add to her original
present, and then of course there was the girls'
contribution. They had bought him a leather wallet
from their combined savings, and on impulse Claire
had taken them both to have their photographs
taken wearing their new velvet dresses.

In addition to the large photograph which she
had had framed and which was now waiting to be
unwrapped amongst his other presents, were two
individual small ones, just the right size to go in his
wallet.

She held her breath as he opened their present,
but she needn't have worried; his reaction was
everything that was necessary to delight both girls.

It took another hour for them to fight the way
through the rest of their presents, while Claire
tidied up and collected the discarded wrappings.

She had kept back the filing system she had
bought for Jay until last. He had already opened the
Roger and Gallet toilet water she had bought him
and unwrapped the navy jacquard sweater with its
design in olive and maroon, and she held her breath
as he now unwrapped her last gift.

For a moment the expression on his face confused
her. He looked so strange that she wondered if she
had somehow angered him.

'If you don't like it . . .' she began, tentatively, but
he shook his head.

'I love it,' he said simply. 'Come here.'

She got up unsteadily, wondering what it was he wanted. Was he perhaps going to kiss her, the way he had done the girls? Her heart thudded shakily at the prospect, but when she reached him, although he took hold of her hand, it was just to tug her down beside him.

'Here's my present to you,' he said softly, handing her a long rectangular parcel.

Claire frowned. She had already received several presents from him, including one of perfume, and an American cookery book, that a brief glance had told her she was going to enjoy. There had also been a much coveted decorators' directory she had glimpsed in the window of an exclusive book shop in Bath, and, rather surprisingly, a silky camisole in softest peach, lavishly trimmed with lace.

'Open it!' demanded Lucy impatiently.

All they had left to open were their large presents, hidden behind the tree, and so, bemusedly, Claire started to unwrap her gift. Inside the paper was a dark leather-covered jewellers' box edged in gold. Claire felt her stomach clench in shock as she fumbled with the fastening and got it open. On the bed of dark velvet lay a necklet of milky pearls, supporting a heart-shaped emerald surrounded by diamonds. It was the most exquisite thing she had ever seen, and she touched it tentatively, too stunned for words.

'Jay ... it's ...' She looked up at him and swallowed. 'You shouldn't have bought me this! It must have cost a fortune!'

'The emerald reminded me of you,' he said quietly. 'Cool, and as clear and honest as a mountain spring that refreshes and revives. Beautiful and rare.' He saw she was about to interrupt and said softly, 'You are all those things to me, Claire, and if it had cost ten times what it did, it still wouldn't be adequate recompense for all that you've done.'

Recompense. She tasted the word and found it bitter. She didn't want to be recompensed. She wanted . . . she wanted to be loved, she realised shockingly, unaware that her face had lost all its colour, or that her eyes had a blind terror in their depths.

She heard Jay's sharply indrawn breath, but didn't connect it with her own reaction to his gift, and then Lucy was saying excitedly, 'Aren't you going to kiss him, Mummy?' And somehow, reacting automatically, she was touching her cold lips to his warm skin, and feeling his sharp recoil with a pain that hurt so much, she couldn't believe she had ever thought she had known pain before.

It was a relief to escape to the kitchen to see to the lunch. Jay took the girls outside on their new sledge, while she worked like an automaton, wondering why it was that she should be condemned to loving a man who could give her only gratitude. And he wouldn't even want to give her that, if he knew the truth. In that moment she knew that she must conceal for ever how she felt about him. If she didn't . . . if she didn't their marriage would be a nightmare. He wouldn't divorce her for the girls' sake, but if she told him how she felt she would lose his friendship, lose those precious confidences he gave her, those evenings together when he talked to her about his work, when she felt as though they met as equals. She would lose all that, without any hope of ever gaining what she really wanted. And

what did she want? For him to love her, yes, but
how—in the way that he loved the girls, or in the
way that he had loved his first wife?

Did she want his tenderness or his passion? She
didn't know, she had only known in that blinding
moment of revelation that she loved him totally.

CHAPTER NINE

'WELL, here we are, ladies—Dallas!'

The faint air of constraint that had sprung up between them after Christmas Day still lingered, despite her forcedly cheerful attempts to dispel it and appear normal, and Claire couldn't help noticing how careful Jay was not to touch her as they disembarked from the plane that had brought them from Heathrow.

She didn't think Jay had actually guessed how she felt about him, but she knew that he sensed something. She often found him watching her in an assessing, almost withdrawn way. Assessing and finding wanting, perhaps? A cold fear dug icy fingers into the pit of her stomach.

'Are you all right?' he queried.

'Just getting used to feeling firm ground underneath my feet again.'

The Goldbergs had sent a chauffeur-driven car to pick them up, and as they drove from the airport and through the city itself Jay pointed out several landmarks to them. It was the flatness of the countryside and the expected and yet awesome vastness of everything that she noticed most, Claire thought as she listened to the girls' excited chatter.

She knew that the Goldbergs owned a house on the outskirts of Dallas and that it was here that Jay's firm had done the work which had won them the contract for John Goldberg's prestigious building developments.

The Goldberg house was built in what Jay had described as a Neo-Colonial style, and featured a large enclosed patio in the manner of the French Creole houses of St Louis. Claire was looking forward to seeing it, but the ten-foot-high brick wall and the security guard on the gates came as rather an unpleasant shock. The man was cordiality itself as he let them through, but Claire couldn't repress a small shiver as she noticed the gun he was wearing.

'John's a millionaire,' Jay told her quietly, 'and these days I'm afraid that means taking certain security precautions.'

Claire knew that the Goldbergs had two almost grown-up children: a son at Yale and a daughter at Vassar.

The long drive curved through immaculately kept gardens, with sprinkler systems to keep the lawns green and fresh, and the house stood at the end of the drive, its long, symmetrical windows gazing out over the grounds.

A double flight of marble steps led up to the colonnaded Palladian-style entrance. The car stopped, and the chauffeur opened the doors. Claire noticed how subdued the girls were as the four of them climbed the steps.

'I had no idea it would be so big!' she whispered to Jay as they approached the front door.

She just had time to catch his grin, and to hear him whisper in a mock American drawl, 'Honey, this is Texas,' before the massive double doors were opened.

The couple who came out to greet them could have starred in any glamorous American soap opera. John Goldberg was tall, his face tanned, his hair just touched with distinguished wings of silver. Celeste Goldberg was petite and blonde. Her silk pants and top shrieked Milan, and there could be no doubting that those pearl and diamond earrings she was wearing were real. Even so, her smile of welcome was warm and genuine, her manner towards the girls, instantly putting them at ease.

They were ushered into a rectangular hallway; a flight of marble steps at the far end rose to a galleried landing. The soft, green-washed walls were embellished with gilded plasterwork, which Claire instantly recognised.

'It looks wonderful!' she told Jay impulsively.

'We certainly think so,' said Celeste. 'And so do all our friends. We've given you a suite of rooms overlooking the patio; I'll show you to them now. I know you must be tired.'

Claire was. In fact, she was finding it hard to understand why sitting still for so long should be able to induce such numbing exhaustion.

'It's this way.'

Claire and the girls followed their hostess upstairs, while Jay lingered to talk to John Goldberg. At the top of the stairs a pair of double doors in white and gold opened out on to a galleried walkway that went all the way round an unroofed quadrangle.

'All the bedrooms have access to the pool and patio area from this gallery,' Celeste told Claire, indicating a flight of steps that went down to the ground below.

As she gazed over the iron railings, Claire could see the rich blue shimmer of the pool. Built in a traditional shape, it was ornamented with a piece of marble statuary, and the patio itself was flagged in white marble diamond-shaped tiles, interspersed with smaller dark blue ones to match the tiles in the pool. White marble columns supported the walkway and a wide variety of exotic climbing plants curled green tendrils around them. The whole effect was one of cool richness, right down to the birds Claire could not see, but could hear singing.

'It's a recording,' Celeste told her, laughing when Claire commented on it. 'John wanted to create the old St Louis-style family patio, but I drew the line at caged birds, so this was a compromise. We do have a much larger pool and barbecue area in the grounds, of course; but we only use it when we're having large parties. John had a tented pavilion area made next to it where we can put down a dance floor and serve a buffet. Ah—this is your suite here.'

She was way, way out of her depth here, realised Claire, marvelling at her hostess's casual acceptance of her possessions and life-style.

Celeste opened a door. 'I've given you two rooms, and a small sitting-room.'

All three rooms were decorated with French Empire-style furnishings and fitments; all three were luxurious and glamorous, as were the two *en suite* bathrooms, but it was not the luxury of her surroundings that made Claire go tense with shock; it was the realisation that Celeste had given her and Jay a bedroom that possessed an enormous king-sized bed.

The girls' room had two twins, but she could hardly suggest that she and Jay sleep in there, and there was certainly no question of anyone sleeping on the delicate chaise-longue at the bottom of the bed.

'Dolores will unpack for you; she and her family have been looking after us for the last ten years. It was Thomas, her son, who drove you here. We don't have dinner until eight, and you'll want to rest before then. Shall I send up some tea for you now, and leave you to settle in?'

Claire was too strung up now to rest, so she shook her head. 'I'm tired,' she admitted, 'but if I let the girls sleep now, they'll never want to go to bed.'

'Well, if I'm any judge, the men will be talking business in John's den. We'll go down there and rout them out, and then we'll have tea in the courtyard. The air-conditioning keeps it lovely and cool, and the fact that it's enclosed protects it from the dreadful winds we get here.'

As they went back downstairs, Claire learned that this evening they would be dining alone with their host and hostess, but that for the rest of their stay the Goldbergs planned to entertain and introduce them to several of their friends.

'John is so thrilled with the work Jay has done for him. Initially he was worried that such a small company wouldn't have the manpower to cope with a large contract, but Jay's dedication and know-how has finally convinced him. I think it was the news that Jay had remarried that finally convinced him,' Celeste added with a brief sideways look at Claire. 'John is a keen advocate of the benefits of a secure and strong marriage. I think it's very romantic how the two of you met and married.' She looked meaningfully at Lucy and Heather, who were preceding them down the stairs. 'And anyone can see how happy those two little girls are. I scarcely recognised Heather. She used to be such an unhappy, withdrawn child.'

'You've met Heather before?'

'Only briefly, when John and I were visiting London. Jay invited us back to the house for drinks, only when we got there it was plain that Susan wasn't at all pleased. Poor Jay—I felt terribly embarrassed for him, and we weren't really surprised when he heard that they'd split up, but John believes that divorce has a very unsettling effect on a man; it stops him from concentrating totally on business.' Celeste added the last few words with a wry grimace. 'I'm afraid my husband is something of a workaholic, but having said that, I wouldn't swop him for anyone else. Come on, we'll go and rout them out of John's den.'

As she listened to the conversation flowing around her, Claire could see what Celeste meant about John being a workaholic, but at least he did not, as many men did, presume that because they were female they could have no conceivable interest or worthwhile comments to add to the conversation, and she could see that he valued Celeste's opinion.

It had been rather a shock to hear Celeste describing their marriage as 'romantic'. Did she think that she and Jay were wildly in love, then? Obviously she must do. Even more disquieting, though, had been her innocent revelations about John's views on men and marriage. Was it possible that Jay had married her not just for Heather's benefit, but possibly for his own?

It was too late by a long time to start querying his motives now, she told herself, and anyway, what did it really matter? It mattered because, having discovered that she loved him, she found that it hurt to think that to him their marriage was just a sensible business manoeuvre. She had thought, before Christmas, that there was a closeness developing between them, a closeness which she had foolishly cherished.

'I think I'll take the girls upstairs now. It's gone six o'clock and they're both beginning to look tired.'

'They'll want something to eat . . .' began Celeste, but Claire shook her head. 'No, the sandwiches they've just eaten and the food they had on the plane will be enough. If they have another meal now, they won't sleep.'

'I'll come and give you a hand.' Jay smiled easily at John Goldberg. 'I miss out so often on saying goodnight to them that I like to share their bedtime whenever I can.'

'Yes, they grow up all too quickly,' John Goldberg agreed. 'I often regret that I didn't have more time to spare for our two when they were kids.'

Claire was surprised by Jay's behaviour. After all, this was essentially a business trip, even if the Goldbergs had specially wanted him to bring his family to meet them, and she had expected Jay to remain downstairs taking to John while she got the girls into bed.

She said as much as they went to their suite, careful to keep her voice down so that Lucy and Heather wouldn't overheard her.

'We're here for four days,' Jay pointed out. 'Plenty of time to discuss business matters, and besides, John's already told me that his advisers have finally agreed the contract. I'm not the sort of man who wants to sacrifice everything on the altar of material success, Claire. Oh, I enjoy my work: I like producing something that I know is good, and I like the success of selling it—but it isn't the be-all and end-all of my existence. I don't want either Lucy or Heather growing up thinking of me as a casual participant in their lives who can be relied on for expensive presents and not much else. Parenting is a dual role.'

They had reached the outer door to their suite. Claire hung back while the two girls rushed eagerly inside. Reluctantly she followed them.

'Jay . . .' she began.

'Mmm?'

'Celeste has only given us one room—with a double bed.'

His eyebrows lifted, and he asked in amusement, 'For all four of us?'

Claire could feel the hot colour flooding betrayingly over her skin. 'No, of course not.'

'Don't worry about it.' Suddenly for some reason his voice sounded clipped, angry almost. 'If I know anything about American beds, it will be large enough for us and at least half a dozen bolsters.'

Claire felt her mouth compress. It irritated her that he should be able to treat the matter so casually, and yet, what had she expected? Horror at the thought of having to share the bed with her? Pleasure?

'Mummy, come and look—this bath is big enough for Lucy *and* me!'

Distractedly Claire pushed aside her disturbing thoughts and went through to the girls' bathroom.

'No, truly, I couldn't eat another mouthful.'

In point of fact, she was totally exhausted, realised Claire, as she refused another helping of sweet. Jet-lag was obviously catching up with her. In contrast the other three, including Jay, all seemed unfairly wide awake.

Not even two cups of coffee in the white and gold drawing-room that overlooked the sweep of lawns at the front of the house could lighten her heavy eyelids, and Jay, catching sight of her smothering yet another yawn, said quietly, 'Why don't you go up to bed? John and I still have one or two things to discuss, and I can see that you're tired.'

'Yes, please don't stand on ceremony, honey,' insisted Celeste, 'and don't worry about having a lie-in in the morning. We've all suffered from jet-lag at one time or another, and we all know what it's like.'

Having been assured that her host and hostess wouldn't think her rude, Claire went gratefully upstairs. She was so tired she could barely walk.

She almost fell asleep in the bath, a huge affair with an in-built jacuzzi effect that she was too exhausted to try.

It was sheer luxury to find that all their luggage had been unpacked and put away. After a couple of attempts she managed to locate her nightdress—in the same drawer as Jay's silk pyjamas—and ridiculously, her last muddled thought as sleep claimed her was to wonder on which side of the bed Jay preferred to sleep. Well, it was too bad if she had chosen the wrong one, she thought grumpily; he would just have to wake her up.

He did, but only very briefly and only because she was an extremely light sleeper.

It was the bedroom door opening that brought her out of a strangely confused dream to the odd knowledge that she was feeling extremely cold. She said as much, very crossly, to Jay as he apologised for waking her, and heard him laugh.

'It's probably the air-conditioning—it's still on, and the temperature does drop quite a lot at night.'

She was almost asleep by the time he came out of the bathroom, one small part of her registering the fact that he was sliding into bed beside her.

As though he sensed her awareness of him, he said calmly, 'Go back to sleep, Claire, there's nothing to be afraid of . . .'

Nine-tenths asleep, she mumbled back, 'I'm not afraid, I'm cold.'

He laughed again, and the sound held a faint hint of indulgent affection. 'If you were the little girl you sound like I could cuddle you until you get warm, but . . .'

He caught her sharply indrawn breath.

'Claire, what is it? You surely don't think I . . .'

'The last person to cuddle me was my father, and then he died, and . . .' She was wide awake now, shivering with a mixture of cold and pain.

She heard the noise Jay made deep in his throat—somewhere between a growl and a groan—and she felt him move, but didn't know why, until she felt her body being turned and held close to his own, one arm holding her gently, while his free hand stroked the nape of her neck comfortingly.

'Part of you is still a frightened little girl, isn't it? Poor little Claire!'

She wasn't a little girl, and it was ridiculous for him to assume that she wanted him to treat her as such. She wanted to be strong and cool, and to push him away, to freeze him off, and make him regret that he had dared to trespass into her most private feelings, and yet the way he was holding her, comforting her, brought back memories so long suppressed. This was what she had craved and

longed for after her parents' death—someone to
hold and comfort her—but there had been no one,
no one at all, and then afterwards . . . after . . . him
. . . the thought of anyone touching her had been so
abhorrent that she had forgotten that she had ever
felt like this.

Instinctively, without being aware of it, she
snuggled closer to him, unaware of his sharp intake
of breath, or the tension invading his body. He felt
warm and safe, and he smelled . . . nice . . . she
thought woollily, burying her face against his skin
and breathing in the scent of it with the voluptuous
innocence of a small child. He was only wearing
pyjama bottoms, and she liked the sensation of his
flesh beneath her hand, where it rested against his
chest. She wriggled closer.

'Claire . . .' She froze as Jay moved away from
her, his hands clamping round her wrists. 'I'm
sorry—I shouldn't have touched you.' His voice was
hard and remote.

What he meant was that he didn't want her to
touch him. Claire's face burned as she realised what
she had done. Instantly she retreated to the other
side of the bed, feeling as bruised and rejected as
only a woman in love can feel when the man she
loves physically repulses her.

'Claire . . . Look, let's talk about this.'

She heard the tentative, gentle note of enquiry in
his voice but ignored it. She wasn't in the mood to
have a reasoned discussion on what had happened.

The very fact that Jay thought it was something
they could talk reasonably about was enough. If he
had been here in bed with Susie . . . The instant the
treacherous thought formed she tried to suppress it,
but it was too late. Jealousy seared her, leaving her

raw and vulnerable, prey to emotions she had never known existed. Despite her exhaustion it was hours before she finally fell asleep.

When she woke up the sun was shining and she was alone. She glanced at her watch and blinked. Half past ten. She really had overslept.

She got up and padded through into the girls' room. It was empty. They must all be downstairs. Putting clean clothes and underwear on the bed she went through into the bathroom, shedding both her nightdress and her robe. She was just about to step into the shower when she saw it. The most enormous spider she had ever seen! And it had seen her—she was convinced of it, convinced that it was staring at her with malevolent glee.

She opened her mouth and screamed in pure panic-reaction, totally unable to drag her attention away from the soft, pulsating body and horrid mass of hairy legs.

Her scream had been pure instinct, and the last thing she had expected was for the bathroom door to be flung open.

'Claire? Ah . . . I see . . . It's all right, come on.'

She was hardly conscious of Jay's hand on her arm as he gently tugged her out of the bathroom and back into the bedroom. It was only when he closed the door, firmly locking the spider inside that she actually dared to breathe again. Jay released her, but she clung to him, shaking.

'It's all right. I just want to get your robe for you.'

For the first time she became conscious that she was naked, and her whole body turned a delicate shade of pink as Jay stepped away from her and then turned to look at her.

There was something strangely driven, reluctant almost in the way he studied her naked body. No doubt compared to Susie she was very ordinary indeed, but there was nothing wrong with the smooth suppleness of her skin, she thought proudly and her waist was narrow enough for Jay to span with both his hands if he wanted to do so. Her breasts weren't particularly large, but they were firm.

She forgot why they were here like this as Jay stared at her; a curious and very intense ache throbbed through her body. Her nipples swelled and hardened into deeply rosy nubs of flesh.

Jay was watching her with a darkly intense absorption. Her stomach muscles fluttered a nervous protest, and she touched startled fingertips to her skin.

'Claire, for God's sake!'

Jay's harsh protest exploded into the silence engulfing them. She looked at him with innocent, hesitant eyes, caught up in a mass of conflicting sensations and emotions.

His face was flushed, his eyes glittering between narrowed lashes. He swallowed, and she followed the movement of his throat, seeing the tiny beads of perspiration dampening his skin. His shirt was open at the throat, revealing a dark tangle of soft hair.

'Claire . . .' His voice was tight with anger; and rough with something else; a kind of raw, aching pain that caught at her heart strings and made her move towards him with the jerky, mechanical gait of a doll, without being aware that she had moved, only knowing that his pain was something she must soothe.

She reached him and wondered at the expression in his eyes, and while she was assimilating it, he reached for her with a tortured, smothered sound, dragging her into his arms, and imprisoning her against his body, so that she felt its heat and its maleness as his mouth moved hotly over her face, communicating a blind, frantic urgency that seemed to echo the fierce throb of her flesh.

No one had ever held her like this before, ever kissed her like this before, and it was like being cast adrift in an alien sea which swelled and roared as it threatened to drown her. There was only Jay to cling to for safety, her nails biting into his skin, as she trembled and shook with a kaleidoscope of new sensations.

Jay's mouth covered hers, hot with urgency. Her eyes widened in shock and she felt him check, and then his hand was in her hair, his fingers spreading against her scalp, his tongue pressing against the closed line of her mouth, until with a suppressed sound of frustration he nipped sharply at her bottom lip.

Her sharp cry of pain surprised them both. Claire almost felt him do a double-take as the glittering heat died out of his eyes and tension invaded his body.

His face was still flushed, but this time with anger.

'Hell, Claire, I'm sorry. I don't know what came over me.' He released her as carefully as though she was made of precious crystal, and then stepped back from her.

He turned round looking for her robe, and she heard him say in a muffled voice, 'For a moment I forgot that . . .'

'That I wasn't Susie?' She felt as though her blood had turned to ice. No, not ice—if she was frozen she wouldn't be feeling this appalling, unendurable pain. In one brief, illuminating moment she had known all that Jay could have given her if he loved her, but he didn't love her. She was merely his wife. His second wife.

She took her robe from him and pulled it on, turning her back on him so that he wouldn't see the agony in her eyes.

'I'll dispose of the spider and then I'll leave you to get dressed. We're all down by the pool.'

It took her almost an hour to get ready to face everyone. She knew that from now on whenever she looked at her naked body she would be imagining Jay's hands on it, Jay's mouth. She shuddered deeply, aware for the first time in her life of the depth and intensity of her own feelings.

The terror of coming face to face with that horrendous spider—she had always feared and loathed them—seemed to have broken loose the chains that had held her in captivity to her sexual fears. She couldn't really explain to herself why it was one minute she loathed anything to do with sex and the next she ached for Jay to be her lover—or had it really happened as quickly as that? Hadn't she slowly been drifting towards this for quite some time, since the start of their marriage, in fact, like a leaf borne unknowingly towards the brink of a weir it didn't know existed?

She couldn't stay here all day, she reminded herself. Sooner or later she would have to face Jay.

'I liked it very much in Dallas, Mummy, but I'm glad we're going home now, are you?'

They were circling Heathrow, and soon their jet would land. Absently responding to Heather's question, Claire glanced at Jay. He was sitting on the opposite side of the aisle, looking out of the window. Since that dreadful episode in their room, he seemed to have withdrawn from her almost completely. He was so cold towards her, so meticulously polite, chilly and indifferent, that she ached sometimes to elicit some response from him, even if that response was only anger.

She had been glad that the Goldbergs had organised so many social events for them, otherwise she didn't know how she would have got through the visit. It had been torture sharing that enormous bed with Jay each night, knowing he was there so close to her, and yet knowing that he did not want her.

Claire had learned a lot about herself in the last few days. She had learned, for instance, that she was a woman who liked to touch. She ached to touch Jay. To run her fingertips over his body, to find out if that dark tangle of body hair felt as silky as it looked. She found herself looking at his mouth sometimes, and wishing she could feel its hard warmth against her own, against . . . against all of her, she admitted, shuddering faintly as she felt the molten heat run through her body.

She had learned something else. She had learned that she was a masochist; she must be, otherwise she would not torture herself with these haunting images of what could never be. Jay did not even desire her, never mind love her, she knew that—and she also knew that what had happened in the past had made it impossible for her to give herself to a man without mutual love. She wanted Jay's love;

she wanted it emotionally, mentally and physically. She wanted the moon. She looked down at Heather who was sitting next to her, and saw trusting eyes looking back at her from the little round face. A wave of love cramped through her: Jay's child. How she would love to give Jay another child. She bent down and gently kissed Heather's dark head. The little girl hugged her back in wordless communication.

'Why are you looking so sad, Mummy?'

Trust sharp-eyed Lucy to notice!

'Oh, I'm not sad,' she lied, 'I'm just thinking.'

'We'll have to go back to school next week, won't we?' Lucy chattered on, and Claire forced herself to listen, glad of the diversion and yet resenting the way Lucy turned confidingly to Jay, confident of his interest and his care. She was actually jealous of her own child! Bitterness rose in her throat and she had to look away.

The last thing she had expected when she married Jay was that she would fall in love with him. Fate had played a very cruel trick on her indeed.

CHAPTER TEN

'CLAIRE, after dinner tonight, when the children are in bed, I'd like to talk to you.'

Over the last two weeks she had barely seen Jay. Ever since their return from Dallas, there had been a kind of armed and guarded tension between them, an atmosphere unlike anything she had experienced before, but which set her nerves on edge so much that she was steadily losing weight.

Jay didn't look too good either, she noticed, turning to look at him. She had avoided doing that recently; it hurt too much. Now she saw that there were deep grooves of tiredness carved along his face, and that his tan had faded, leaving him looking almost sallow. Of course he had been working hard—and late almost every night. They were busy, but she also knew that he stayed away because he didn't want to come home.

What had happened to the comfortable, pleasant relationship they had been building up before they went to Dallas? Her love had happened to it, that was what. She had fallen in love with him, and now she was unable to let herself relax with him because she was mortally afraid of what she might betray.

But it wasn't just she who had changed. Jay had changed too: he had become remote and withdrawn. Sometimes she found him watching her with a brooding expression in his eyes, and she thought she knew the reason. Whatever he might have said to her, or told himself, he still loved Susie, and it had been that day when he held her in his arms and realised that she was not his first wife that he had discovered this. She was convinced of it.

Now, hearing him say that they needed to talk made her heart bump and jolt with shock and fear. What was he going to say to her? She looked at him out of the corner of her eye and saw that his face was wearing the blanked-off, almost bitter look that had become so familiar to her recently.

'They've gone up to have their baths now,' she told him tonelessly. 'They were both tired tonight.'

Even so, it was over an hour before both girls were settled. 'I'll go down and make some coffee.'

Jay shook his head. 'I'll do that. You do enough.' His mouth compressed slightly. 'You go and sit down.'

She was too nervous to sit down, and instead she paced the sitting-room floor nervously. Next week the workmen were due to start; she had shown Jay the colour schemes she sad chosen, but his response had been abstracted and remote. Perhaps he was regretting giving her *carte blanche* with the décor, and that was what he wanted to talk to her about. Perhaps he had now decided that he wanted the house to remain as it was—as Susie had decorated it.

When he came in with the coffee, Claire was staring unseeingly out of one of the windows.

'Come and sit down.' His voice sounded rough and he looked tense. 'Please come and sit down, Claire,' he amended, mistaking the reason for her frozen stance. He ran impatient fingers through his hair and added rawly, 'This is bad enough as it is.

When we married I made you certain promises and . . .'

'And now you're having second thoughts.' She marvelled at her own calm. How cool and controlled she sounded; she was really quite proud of herself. Inwardly she was awash with intense pain and agony. She knew now what Jay wanted to say to her; he wanted to tell her that their marriage wasn't working out, that he couldn't live with her any more because she wasn't Susie.

'How did you *know*?' He was frowning heavily and looked pale. 'I thought I'd . . .'

'Hidden how you feel?' She smiled mirthlessly. 'Some things can't be hidden, Jay.'

'I see.' His voice was heavy. 'I hadn't realised you'd guessed how I felt. Well, since you have, what do you suggest we do about it?'

'What do *I* suggest? She stared at him. 'There's nothing I can do, Jay.'

For a moment he just stared back at her, and then his face tightened and he was walking towards her, quickly and almost menacing, his whole body taut with tension.

When his fingers curled round her arm she tried to jerk away, but he wouldn't release her. Instead he shook her, the aura of suppressed violence emanating from him so totally alien to his normal manner that she couldn't take it in properly.

'*Nothing* you can do? Nothing you *will* do, don't you mean?' he grated bitterly. 'For God's sake, Claire, you must know what it's doing to me living with you like this!'

'Of course I know! Do you think I can't see the changes in you? But what can I do? I can't bring her back for you, Jay! I can't be Susie.'

'Susie?' He released her so quickly that she half stumbled against the sofa. 'What the hell are you talking about?'

His face had gone white with rage, the anger glittering in his eyes making her take a step back.

'Jay, you know what I'm talking about. I'm talking about the fact that you're having second thoughts about our marriage because you've discovered you still love Susie.'

There was a long, long silence and then, speaking slowly and spacing the words out as though he was having the greatest difficulty in forming the words, Jay said thickly, 'I don't believe I'm hearing this. Are you for real?' He shook his head. 'You're way, way off beam!'

'But you agreed that you were having second thoughts . . .'

'About the *terms* of our marriage, not what happened in the past. I've fallen in love with you, Claire,' he told her flatly, 'and I want you in all the ways a man wants the woman he loves. I want to feel your skin against my hands, I want to touch it with my lips, I want to spread your hair out over my pillow and thread it through my fingers. Just the way you turn your head is enough to burn me up, do you know that? I want this, Claire,' he told her roughly, taking her in his arms and bringing his mouth down hard on the softness of hers.

The kiss took her by surprise, her mouth tremulous and soft beneath his, her tongue retreating shyly from the fierce invasion of his. She could feel his heart thudding furiously against her body. She could feel the tension in him—and the arousal, she acknowledged as she shook with shock and disbelief.

Abruptly his mouth left hers and she was free. Free to stare wide-eyed at him, to touch tremulous fingertips to her mouth. She saw his eyes darken and a hot flush of colour burn along his face, and her stomach lifted and plunged.

'But you can't love me . . .'

'Why not?' he laughed hollowly. 'Because you don't love me? Life isn't like that, Claire.'

'But you didn't love me when you proposed marriage.'

'No,' he agreed, dragging in a lungful of air and fighting for self-control. More calmly he continued, 'No, I didn't, but I did like you very much, both as a woman and as a person. I liked your quick intelligence, your interest in other people, your compassion, your womanliness. A womanliness it seemed a miracle you had kept when I knew what had happened to you. I saw the love and caring you gave Lucy, and I wanted that caring for my own child—and then for myself. After Susie left me I swore I'd never enter a permanent romantic relationship with any woman again. I knew I couldn't put up with the sort of infidelity and cheating I'd had with Susie. It was my own fault; I should never have married her. I should have let her have her abortion and we should have gone our separate ways, but I couldn't believe she meant it. I couldn't believe she didn't want our child. I thought she was just being independent and proud and that really she wanted marriage. I threatened to tell her parents what she was planning to do if she didn't marry me, and she never forgave me for that—or for making her have Heather. When you told me how Lucy was conceived and how you felt about sex I knew you'd never be unfaithful to me. I knew then that I desired you, but I told myself I could control it. It was only later after we were married that I realised I couldn't, and with that realisation came others, like how much happiness and extra dimensionality you'd brought to my life; like how eager I was to come home to you and the girls; before I knew it, I'd made the transition from liking to loving . . .'

'And does loving me mean that you want me physically?' Claire asked him.

His eyes didn't waver. 'Yes,' he said gravely. 'I've already told you that. Wanting you, desiring you . . . those are a part of my love.'

'But in Dallas you pushed me away!'

His eyes narrowed incredulously. 'Pushed you away? For God's sake, Claire, how much self-control do you think I have? You were completely naked, I was holding you in my arms. I wanted to take you to bed right there and then, and show you how I felt about you,' he admitted flatly, adding in a thick and unfamiliar voice, 'although, the way I was feeling, I doubt that I'd have made it as far as the bed!'

She shook visibly with the effect of what he was saying, knowing that he was telling her the truth, but totally unable to take it in.

'What on earth gave you the idea I still loved Susie?'

'The way you rejected me. I thought you were wishing I was her, and then since we got back from Dallas, you've been so distant.'

'So have you,' he pointed out.

'Yes, but . . .'

'But what? Was it because I kissed you, Claire? Did I frighten you so much that you felt you had to keep me at a distance?'

The anguish in his eyes was too much for her to bear.

'I wasn't frightened of you. I was ... I was frightened of myself, Jay, frightened of how you made me feel, of ...'

'How *do* I make you feel?'

He had never looked less urbane and in control, and she had never loved him more, she thought achingly, watching the expressions race across his face: dread ... hope ... need ...

'You make me feel ...' She broke off and licked her lips nervously. She heard him make a strangled sound deep in his chest and looked at him with wide nervous eyes.

'Claire?' His voice pleaded and begged, and promised terrible retribution if she strung out his torment any longer.

'You make me feel like a woman,' she told him huskily. 'You make me ... want you, Jay ... You make me love you.'

There was a long, poignant silence and then he said softly, 'Come here.'

She almost ran into his open arms. They closed round her so tightly she could hardly breathe. He kissed her hungrily, running his tongue over her top lip and then the bottom one, probing their softness.

'Open your mouth.'

She shuddered as his tongue touched hers, but not with revulsion. As he felt her shudder, Jay raised his head, his eyes dark with pain. 'It's too soon, isn't it?' he whispered rawly. 'I'm rushing you too much. God knows I don't want to hurt or frighten you. I want to give you all the time there is. I want to cherish and protect you. I ...'

She knew all that. She also knew gloriously and freely that she wanted him. Here and now at this moment in time, she wanted to be at one with him in a celebration of their love.

Raising herself up on tiptoe, she leaned towards him, cupping his face running her tongue over his top lip in the way he had caressed hers, and then beyond it, feeling the faint prickle of his beard. 'Make love to me, Jay.' She interspersed the words with soft kisses. 'I want to be your wife, to bear your child. I want . . .'

She felt his indrawn breath and shivered heatedly in delight as his mouth opened over hers.

She was drowning in pleasure, floating in a delicious sensuous haze. She felt his hands on her body, and made a soft sound of satisfaction as he stripped it free of clothes. Her breasts filled his hands as though they were made for them, her nipples tight and urgent with desire.

'I think we'd better go upstairs.'

She didn't want to be apart from him, and she twined her arms around him, burying her hot face in his throat, tasting the salt heat of his skin.

'Claire, you're not making this easy for me.'

She didn't listen; she was too busy struggling with the buttons on his shirt. When he helped her with them she murmured a pleased sigh of pleasure, raking her nails gently through the darkness of his chest hair.

It *was* soft. She bent her head and pressed her face against his body. He shuddered and moaned something unintelligible into her ear, his mouth devouring the arched line of her throat and then beyond.

When his lips gently caressed the taut hardness of

her nipple Claire thought she would faint from the pleasure. She clung to him as it coiled through her, unashamedly digging her fingers into his back, her body arching supplicatingly.

Somehow they were lying on the floor, supported by the cushions Jay had dragged off the sofa. The power and beauty of his naked body thrilled and aroused her. His hands stroked her skin and she was filled with a wanton delight, giving herself to him easily and eagerly, twisting and writhing against him as his hands and lips brought her to the edge of ecstasy.

It was she who begged him to enter her, sensing that he was fearful of hurting her, but her body welcomed him joyfully, his mouth absorbing her delirious cries of pleasure as they surged together to the glittering tantalising heights and then finally fell slowly back to earth.

'What are you doing?'

Claire had fallen asleep after they had made love, but now she was awake, watching Jay pick up their discarded clothes. He was wearing a towelling robe and she was covered in a duvet.

'We don't want the girls asking awkward questions, do we?' He abandoned his task and came over to her. 'How *could* you think I still loved Susie?' he groaned against her mouth, taking her in his arms.

'I don't know.' Claire gave him a smile that was purely mischievous. 'Perhaps you ought to convince me again that you don't . . . just to be on the safe side . . . The safe side!' Her face changed, and Jay frowned and stared at her.

'What is it?' he demanded roughly. 'Claire,

what's wrong? *Did* I hurt you after all? Did . . .'

'It's nothing like that. I love you, Jay, and I know you'd never hurt me. It's just . . .'

'What?'

She coloured delicately and offered with a small laugh, 'Well, I've never done this sort of thing before, and . . .'

'And?'

'We didn't take any precautions, Jay. I could have a baby!'

'You said you wanted my child,' he reminded her, watching her.

'I do . . . but you might not . . .'

'Is that what you really think?' he asked thickly. Bending down, he scooped her up into his arms, duvet and all.

'You're right,' he told her. 'I do have to convince you.'

At the top of the stairs Jay paused and, looking down into her glowing face, asked softly, 'Which room, madam, yours or mine?'

'How about ours?' Claire suggested.

'Ours. Mmm. I think I like the idea of that—we'll buy ourselves a new bed, I think, and it won't be ten feet wide! I want you as close to me as it's possible to be from now on. Close to me in all the ways there are, Claire. I've been so lucky to find you . . .'

Fate had not been unkind to her after all, Claire acknowledged headily as he shouldered open his bedroom door and carried her over to the bed.

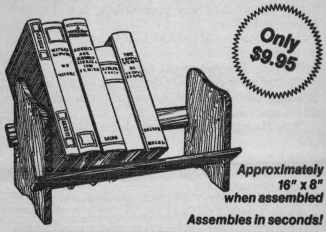

Take 4 books
& a surprise gift
FREE

SPECIAL LIMITED-TIME OFFER

Mail to   **Harlequin Reader Service**®

In the U.S.   In Canada
901 Fuhrmann Blvd.   P.O. Box 609
P.O. Box 1867   Fort Erie, Ontario
Buffalo, N.Y. 14269-1867 L2A 5X3

YES!   Please send me 4 free Harlequin Superromance®
novels and my free surprise gift. Then send me 4 brand-new novels
every month as they come off the presses. Bill me at the low price
of $2.74 each*—a 7% saving off the retail price. There are no
shipping, handling or other hidden costs. There is no minimum
number of books I must purchase. I can always return a shipment
and cancel at any time. Even if I never buy another book from
Harlequin, the 4 free novels and the surprise gift are mine to keep
forever.   134 BPS BP7F

*Plus 49¢ postage and handling per shipment in Canada.

Name	(PLEASE PRINT)
Address	Apt. No.
City	State/Prov. Zip/Postal Code

This offer is limited to one order per household and not valid to present
subscribers. Price is subject to change.   DOSR-SUB-1C

Harlequin Presents

Coming Next Month

Available in June wherever paperback books are sold, or through Harlequin Reader Service:

In the U.S.
901 Fuhrmann Blvd.
P.O. Box 1397
Buffalo, N.Y. 14240-1397

In Canada
P.O. Box 603
Fort Erie, Ontario
L2A 5X3

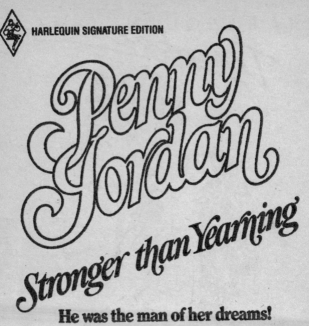

HARLEQUIN SIGNATURE EDITION

Penny Jordan

Stronger than Yearning

He was the man of her dreams!

The same dark hair, the same mocking eyes; it was as if the Regency rake of the portrait, the seducer of Jenna's dream, had come to life. Jenna, believing the last of the Deverils dead, was determined to buy the great old Yorkshire Hall—to claim it for her daughter, Lucy, and put to rest some of the painful memories of Lucy's birth. She had no way of knowing that a direct descendant of the black sheep Deveril even existed—or that James Allingham and his own powerful yearnings would disrupt her plan entirely.

Penny Jordan's first Harlequin Signature Edition *Love's Choices* was an outstanding success. Penny Jordan has written more than 40 best-selling titles—more than 4 million copies sold.

Now, be sure to buy her latest bestseller, *Stronger Than Yearning*. Available wherever paperbacks are sold—in June.